SECRETS

IN THE

ATTIC

This novel is a work of fiction. Situations, scenarios, and characters in this book are a reflection of creative imagination and not representative of any specific person, group, situation, or event.

All scripture quotations, unless otherwise indicated, are taken from the Holy Bible, New International Version®, NIV®. Copyright ©1973, 1978, 1984, 2011 by Biblica, Inc.™ Used by permission of Zondervan. All rights reserved worldwide. www.zondervan.com The "NIV" and "New International Version" are trademarks registered in the United States Patent and Trademark Office by Biblica, Inc.

Cover design by: Irfan B.

Proofreading and editing by Deb Hall with The Write Insight (thewriteinsight.com).

NOTE FROM THE AUTHOR

If you've picked up this book for your child, you can rest in the knowledge that it is Christian, it is clean, and it is filled with valuable lessons. There might be a few moments in this book that will spark your child to come ask you a question for clarification. Be prepared!

There's mischief, there's marshmallows, and there's the magical quality of the unknown and the what-might-be (only without the magic.) I hope you and your little ones have as much fun reading this book as I have had writing it.

With love,
C.C. Warrens

WORDS THAT MAY BE NEW TO YOU

Oma (Oh-ma): German for Grandma

Opa (Oh-pa): German for Grandpa

Liebling (Lee-bling): German for darling

Insufferable (In-suff-er-uh-bull): too hard to deal with

Poltergeist (Pull-tur-guy-st): German for a noisy spirit that knocks things around

Schatzi (Shot-zee): German for treasure, honey, sweetheart

Extraordinaire (ext-roar-din-air): really good at something specific, outstanding

Intrusive (in-true-siv): nosy, asking unwelcome questions, prying

SECRETS

IN THE

ATTIC

STONY BROOKE, KANSAS

1998

The attic door was jammed, glued in place by years of dust and cobwebs, and it groaned but didn't open as Holly leaned against it.

She was nine years old—she hadn't needed help opening a door since she was five—but this one was stubborn.

"Come on," she grunted, digging her sneakers into the step and gripping the glass knob tighter. It twisted partway before catching.

Rats, she thought, releasing the knob.

"I think it's locked."

And she really wanted to see what was behind it. The spooky staircase to the attic had tickled her "curious bone" the moment she saw it. That was what Daddy called it, but she was pretty sure it wasn't a real bone. Unless it was like a funny bone.

1

"Why would Mr. Berkshire lock his attic?"

Holly looked over at Jordan, her best friend, and shrugged. "Maybe he doesn't want other people snooping?"

"He lives here all by himself. It's not like his dog can sneak into the attic when he's not looking."

Old Mr. Berkshire didn't have any family in town, and his only friend was his dog, Rubio. And Rubio wasn't exactly the friendliest dog. When he got all twitchy in his sleep, he was probably dreaming about chomping on someone's ankle.

"He could have expensive stuff up here he doesn't want stolen," Holly said.

Jordan looked up at the peeling wallpaper and burned-out bulb on the ceiling. "Mmm . . . I doubt that."

Yeah, he was probably right.

Holly crouched and brushed the carrot-red bangs back from her face so she could peek through the crack beneath the door. Dust and cobwebs clung to the narrow gap, but she thought she could see the edge of a rug. And what might be a pair of colorful shoes. "What do you think is in there?"

"Mice. And spiders."

Holly blew out a breath, scattering the dust bunnies. "I bet it's full of adventures and secrets. That's why he locks the door. So they can't get out."

"That doesn't make sense."

"Does too."

2

"You can't lock adventures and secrets in an attic, Holly. They're not real things you can pack in boxes."

"I think you can, and I wanna know what they are." Holly squinted, trying to see as much of the room as she could. There were probably whole stacks of exciting things in there. Mr. Berkshire must've done *something* interesting before he got old.

A puff of air blew the dust back toward her, tickling her nose, and she sneezed. Something white drifted past the crack, and Holly sucked in a breath. "What was that?"

Jordan dropped to a crouch beside her. "What?"

"Someone's in the attic," she whispered, in case the *someone* could hear them.

"But the door's locked. Why would Mr. Berkshire lock someone in?"

"Maybe they did something bad, and the attic is like . . . a time-out spot."

"Nah, he's too nice. Plus, there are spiderwebs over the keyhole." He pointed to the lock on the door.

"So?"

"So that means no one's unlocked it in a long time. Like months, probably. When was the last time you were in time-out for that long?"

Holly thought about that. "Yesterday."

"*Yesterday* you were in time-out for *months*?"

"It felt like months."

"What did you do?"

3

"Gin and I were having a parade in the house, and I was doing cartwheels after Mom told me not to," she explained.

"You broke something, didn't you?"

"Only a little something." But that tiny vase broke into more pieces than the huge puzzle of the United States Daddy had built and framed on the living room wall. "It was an accident. But Mom made me sit on the couch and be quiet for twenty whole minutes anyway. That's forever." She'd felt like she was going to explode from too much energy by the time Mom said she could get up.

"Well, I don't think Mr. Berkshire put anyone in his attic for time-out."

Holly puckered her lips to one side in thought. "I guess it could've been a ghost." With the spiderwebs over the keyhole, that was probably it.

"There's no such thing as ghosts, Holly."

"You don't know that."

Jordan did that thing with his face where he looked at her like a grown-up who thought her imagination was too big. But he wasn't a grown-up. He wasn't even a full year older than her. "They're made up. Just like the Watcher Tree."

Holly wasn't so sure about that.

The Watcher Tree might be a legend, but ghosts weren't just some silly kids' story. Plenty of grown-ups believed they were real. Even the Bible mentioned a ghost, so that meant they *had* to be real, didn't it?

4

"Timmy says spooky spirits like to hang around in old attics," Holly said. "He says he saw one once, and it looked like the pictures his family has of his grandpa. He talked to him and everything."

"Timmy has a new story every day of school."

That was true. Sometimes it was hard to tell if he was being honest or not.

"Oma says people who tell stories all the time are usually making them up, and they're gonna be one of two things when they grow up," Jordan said.

"What two things?"

"I didn't pay attention to that part, but Timmy's definitely gonna be one of them."

Probably a book writer, Holly thought. They made up stories all the time. "What are you gonna be when you grow up?" Holly asked.

"Dad wants me to come work at the sheriff's department with him, but that sounds boring. I'd rather be a professional football player."

Professional football sounded more boring than being a sheriff, in Holly's opinion.

"I'm gonna be an explorer," she said. "I wanna go everywhere and see everything. Like the colored lights in Alaska and the castles Oma told us about in Germany. Someday I wanna be a vet like Mom, but traveling first."

Jordan frowned, like her answer bothered him. "You wanna leave Stony Brooke?"

5

"Holly, Jordan! Where did you two sneak off to? You're supposed to be wiping down the kitchen cabinets."

Holly gasped at the sound of her mom's voice and snatched up her cleaning rag. She dashed down the attic steps with Jordan on her heels, down the second set of steps to the first floor, and skidded into the kitchen. Jordan bumped into her and nearly sent her tumbling into Mom, who stood there with her hands on her hips.

"Here we are," Holly announced brightly.

Mom's eyes—the same honey brown as Holly's—narrowed with suspicion. "I recognize that scramble. It's the we-almost-got-caught-doing-something-we-shouldn't-be-doing scramble. What were you two up to?"

Holly glanced at Jordan. They couldn't lie, even if they wanted to. Mom denied having any superpowers, but Holly would bet her last marshmallow Peep that Mom could read people's minds. She always seemed to know things no one told her.

Holly twisted the cleaning rag nervously in her hands. "We were cleaning, really, but then we got, um . . ."

"Distracted," Jordan said.

Mom didn't look surprised. "Helping Mr. Berkshire was your idea, Holly."

Guilt squirmed in Holly's stomach. "I know."

They were here to help clean old Mr. Berkshire's house. He had a bad heart, and the doctors told him not

6

to do anything to put stress on it. He couldn't clean his home or mow his grass, so Holly's family was helping.

"Can you work on the kitchen without me here to keep you focused?" Mom asked.

Holly looked at the floor and nodded. "I'm sorry I got distracted."

Mom crouched in front of her so she could look her in the face. "Everyone gets distracted sometimes, honey. Even adults. But what's important is that when we agree to help someone, we do it to the best of our ability. And we do it with a cheerful heart. Remember why you wanted to help Mr. Berkshire?"

"Because he's old and lonely, and no one's cared about him or loved him in a long time, and no one should feel that way."

"Imagine how loved he will feel knowing that you cheerfully gave your time and energy for him. He'll feel so loved, he might burst."

"And then we'll have to clean that up too," Jordan said, then snickered when Holly's mom frowned at him. "Just kidding."

Mom shook her head and stood. "Go be cheerful. Both of you. We'll leave in an hour and come back tomorrow morning."

"Okay," Holly and Jordan said at the same time.

Before Jordan could speak, Holly blurted, "Pinch, poke, you owe me a Cherry Coke."

"You can have all the cherry. It tastes like cough syrup."

"Does not." Cherry was the best. Cherry soda, cherry suckers, cherry Jolly Ranchers. Even red licorice was tasty, and it only sort of tasted like cherries.

Holly rubbed her rag along the creases of the cupboards, wiping away the dust. Some of it was so thick and crusted in place that it made her fingers hurt trying to scrub it away.

The mower rumbled to life outside, and Holly peered through the dirty window to see Daddy pushing it. She sighed, disappointed she wasn't allowed to do that part. Someday she would be big enough.

Humming drew Holly's attention back to the kitchen. Gin, her identical twin sister, bounced into the room, the heels of her sneakers flashing red with every step. "Can I help dust? I'm a good duster."

Gin was a terrible duster. Worse than Holly even. She got distracted by everything and then forgot what she was supposed to be doing. That was because something went sideways when she was born and the doctors said Gin's brain would never work like everyone else's.

"Mom said you had to pick up everything on the living room floor so she can sweep," Holly reminded her.

"I did. I even found a piece of candy." Gin stuck out her tongue with the melting sliver of candy on it. "See?"

"That's gross, Gin," Jordan said. "You're not supposed to eat stuff off the floor."

Holly held out her hand. "Spit it out."

Gin sucked her tongue back into her mouth with a pout. "I don't wanna spit it out. I found it."

"The floor is dirty."

Gin twisted the skirt of her dress as she struggled to come up with something to say. "Oma says a little dirt, um, dirt didn't ever hurt nobody, so . . . it's okay. And it doesn't taste dirty."

"You have to spit it out, Gin-Gin," Holly said.

"No!" Gin slapped both hands over her mouth and ran back into the living room.

Holly chased after her, following her out the front door onto the porch, but Gin took off around the house toward the backyard. "Gin!"

"She's a quick one," Mr. Berkshire said. He sat on a bench, sipping water from a beat-up metal cup. His long, scraggly beard hung down into his lap, and his long legs stretched across the porch to touch the railing.

"She's not supposed to run with candy in her mouth. She got it stuck in her throat once, and Daddy had to squeeze it out of her."

"That don't sound too pleasant." He patted the bench beside him. "Come keep me company for a minute."

Holly fidgeted with her towel. "Mom said I'm supposed to be cleaning."

9

"You can take a break to chat with an old man. Your mom won't mind."

"If you're wrong and she puts me in time-out again, you have to get me out of it, or I'll explode."

"You have yourself a deal."

Holly shuffled over and plunked down beside him. "Is your heart okay today?"

"My heart is better than okay today. It's nice not to be alone."

"I don't like being alone either. But at least you have Rubio all the time." The dog let out a snore at his name that made his cheeks flap.

"True enough, but between you and me, he don't talk much."

Holly wished animals could talk. Being a vet like her mom and being able to talk to the animals like Dr. Dolittle would be the best thing ever.

When Mr. Berkshire readjusted his beard before taking a drink of his water, Holly asked, "Are you gonna chop off your beard?"

He blinked at her. "Why would I do that?"

"Because you're bald."

"What's your point?"

"You could chop it off and make a wig."

Mr. Berkshire burst out laughing.

Holly crossed her arms, anger fizzling in her belly. "What's so funny?" It wasn't like it was a bad idea.

10

Mr. Berkshire cleared his throat. "I meant no offense, little spitfire. But I got no plans to cut my beard and glue it to my forehead. I'll leave it right where it is."

"In your cup of water?"

He looked down to see that his beard had dipped into his water while he was laughing. "Heavens to Betsy." He pulled it out and squeezed the water onto the porch. "I suppose I deserve that for laughing at your idea."

"It wouldn't have happened if it was on your head."

"You've got no problem sharing your thoughts, do ya?"

"Nope." She hopped to her feet. "I should go help Jordan clean some more. I don't want Mom to think I got distracted again."

"I appreciate you kids helping out an old man. I know you could be outside playing on a nice day like this, but you're here instead."

"We don't mind helping. Mom and Daddy say it's important to help people when they need it because that's what Jesus did."

"I don't know much about that Jesus character, but I've heard He was kind."

"I can tell you about Him if you want. I know all kinds of stuff about Him from Sunday school."

Mr. Berkshire scratched at his beard. "Maybe some other time."

"Okay." She stepped into the house, then turned back. "Mr. Berkshire, did you know your attic door is stuck shut?"

Sadness crossed his face. "I locked it decades ago. I don't even remember where I put the key."

"Why did you lock it?"

"Because there's nothing up there but old ghosts, and I don't want to let them back into my life. It's better for everyone if they stay locked behind that door."

Holly gasped. She'd been right. The attic *was* haunted.

A real live ghost, Holly thought, possibilities buzzing around in her brain like busy little bumbles. She had so many questions, and the bookstore was the perfect place to find answers.

A metallic squeak drew her eyes upward. The wooden sign for Criss Cross Books, painted with blue and purple stripes, swayed in the afternoon breeze.

"Jordan, unlock the door for me, would you?" Daddy tossed his ring of keys, and Jordan caught them.

"Yes, sir."

Jordan unlocked the glass door while Daddy scooped up the donation box of books sitting below the window. People in town donated all kinds of books, and Daddy stopped by to bring them inside even on days when the bookstore was closed. He didn't want them to get caught in the rain.

A book slid off the uneven pile and fell out of the box, slapping the sidewalk.

"I'll get it, Daddy." Gin picked it up and hugged it to her chest.

"You're a wonderful helper, Gingersnap," Daddy said, walking through the door Jordan held open.

Gin followed, shining as bright as the glow-in-the-dark stars all over their bedroom ceiling. She loved helping, even if she could only do little things.

Holly drew in a deep breath as she stepped inside. She loved Daddy's bookstore. It smelled like all the different books on the shelves. Some of the really old books reminded her of sweet vanilla frosting. Others reminded her of storm cellars, like they'd gotten a little wet and musty before coming here. Sometimes the used books still smelled like the people who owned them before—old lady perfume and cigarette smoke.

Daddy boxed up the worst-smelling books and drove them to the next town to drop them off at a donation center.

Criss Cross Books was too small to keep all the books people dropped off.

Daddy set the latest box on the front counter. "Quite a few donations today. Let's hope there's something good. Who wants to help me go through them?"

Gin's hand shot into the air. "I do!"

"Do you know if Mr. Berkshire likes to read, Holly? We can take him a few books when we go back tomorrow. It's hard to be lonely when you have book friends to spend the evening with."

"He never said."

Daddy pulled the reading glasses from his pocket and slipped them on. "We'll take a few books with us just in case."

"Okay. Me and Jordan are gonna go look for something to read tonight."

"Jordan and I," Daddy corrected. "And go ahead, but don't take too long. I told your mom we wouldn't be late for dinner."

Holly looked at Jordan as they started down the aisle. "Wanna have dinner with us? It's pizza night. Mom says you can come over for dinner whenever you want."

"I'm hanging out with Oma tonight."

Oma was Jordan's grandmother, and she was the best. If Holly could have a grandmother, she would definitely pick Oma.

"What kind of books are we looking for?" Jordan asked.

"Spooky books."

He groaned and dropped his head back. "Not the ghost thing again."

"You might not believe they're real, but I asked Mr. Berkshire why he keeps his attic locked, and he said

15

it's because there are old ghosts up there, and he wants them to stay there."

Jordan's eyes widened. "Really?"

"Yep. So I'm gonna learn as much as I can." She pulled a book from the shelf and flipped through the pages.

It had too many big words she didn't know yet, and she didn't want to spend the whole night looking up words in the dictionary. She hated doing that. She put it back and tried a different one.

"I wonder if this ghost is friendly or mean. Probably mean if he has to lock the door to keep her in," Holly mumbled, thinking out loud.

"How do you know it's a *she*?"

"I saw lady shoes when I peeked under the door, and that white cloth could've been a dress."

"If he said 'ghosts,' plural, wouldn't that mean more than one?"

"That's a good point. There could be a whole ghost family in the attic. I wonder what they do up there all day."

Holly returned another book to the shelf and scanned the titles for a different one. She spotted one on the top shelf, but she was too little to reach it. Where was the step stool? Georgetta, the lady who helped out around the bookstore, was always moving it. Didn't she know she was supposed to put things back where she got them?

"What are you looking for?" Jordan asked.

16

"Something to stand on so I can get that book up there." She pointed to the blue cover. "Can you reach it if you jump?"

Jordan tilted his head as he gauged the distance. "No. That shelf is like nine feet off the floor."

"Can you give me a boost?"

"Why don't we ask your dad to get it?"

"Because we can do it by ourselves. Like we do when we go tree climbing and you help me reach the high branches."

"Mmm . . . I guess we can try that." Jordan sank to a crouch on the floor. "But don't poke me in the eye like last time."

"I won't." Holly stepped over his shoulders and grabbed the edge of the shelf for balance instead of Jordan's head. "Ready."

Jordan straightened his legs slowly, wobbling and staggering in a way that made Holly's stomach go fluttery. She clung tight to the shelves as she climbed higher, seeing everything from a whole new angle.

She looked down at the floor. "Wow."

"Wow what?" Jordan grunted.

"I'm gonna be tall like this someday."

"You're not gonna be seven feet tall."

"You just watch." She reached for the blue book titled *Ghost, Goblins, and Ghouls*, but it was too far to her left. Jordan had stumbled the other way when he was picking her up.

17

He grunted and held tight to her legs. "Hurry up, Holly. You're getting heavy."

"I can't reach it. It's too far left." She stretched as far as she could, throwing off their balance. Jordan stumbled backward, and Holly's fingers slipped from the bookshelf.

Her arms flailed like that whacky, waving, inflatable tube man she saw on TV for the Olympics. Jordan was going to trip over his own feet, and then she would crash to the floor and crack her head open like an egg.

Jordan stumbled forward again, and they both bumped into the bookshelf. Holly grabbed at anything she could hold on to, sending a few books raining to the floor before she managed to grab the back of the open shelf.

Her heart pounded like the whole marching band was inside her body—booming in her chest, drumming in her head, tapping a rhythm in her fingers, and doing a weird flutter-swish in her stomach.

Jordan panted below her. "I knew . . . this was a bad . . . idea. You always . . . have bad ideas."

Holly snatched the book in front of her face. "Got it!"

Jordan bent his knees and leaned forward so she could slide down his back to the floor, but she tumbled off sideways, landing on her butt with an *oomph!*

"Ow. I bruised my butt bone."

Jordan rubbed at his shoulder. "That's your *tail*bone."

"I don't have a tail." Holly pushed to her feet and held up the book with a grin. "We did it." She turned the pages of the book in her hands, searching for the section about ghosts.

Jordan leaned closer to look at the illustrations. "If ghosts are real, why do some look like Casper and others look like real people but like . . . see-through?"

"I'm sure it says if you read the words."

"I don't like reading as much as you do."

Holly didn't understand that at all. Gin didn't read because she couldn't understand a lot of stuff, but Jordan was smart. He could read anything. "How can you not like reading books? They're like a movie in your head."

"My head doesn't do that."

"Oh. Your brain must be really boring."

He scowled. "Maybe *your* brain is boring."

"Nope. Mine's really busy all the time. Mom says it's like a three-ring circus with lions and jugglers and those funny people who walk on ropes in their underwear."

"They're called tightrope walkers, and they don't wear underwear."

Holly looked up from the book. "Why wouldn't they wear underwear?"

"I mean they don't *just* wear underwear. They have clothes over top like everybody else."

Ohhh. That made more sense.

Jordan heaved a sigh and leaned against the bookshelf. "Why don't we ask your dad about ghosts? I bet he would know if they're real or not, and then you wouldn't have to read all this stuff."

Holly had considered that, but she would be ten in seven months—almost grown. "I'm big enough to figure this out on my own." She turned the page, sucked in a breath, and poked a paragraph with her finger. "Jordan, look!"

"I can't look. Your finger's in the way." He moved her hand so he could read what she had. "Ghosts are rumored to haunt places where they lived, died, or were buried. In rare cases, they haunt people."

Holly frowned. "Do you think someone used to live in Mr. Berkshire's attic and when they died, they turned into a ghost? Maybe he keeps the door locked so they can't escape."

"It says 'ghosts are *rumored* to haunt' those places. Oma says rumors are stories people pass around, and we shouldn't believe them 'cause they're usually not true."

A book slid off the shelf beside them and thumped to the floor. Holly's heart backflipped in her chest, and Jordan jumped. How did it move all by itself?

Daddy's bookstore couldn't be haunted, too, could it? Was that why the step stool was always disappearing and why some of the books kept moving to the wrong shelves?

Another book thumped to the floor, followed by a giggle.

Holly peered into the opening and found her sister grinning back from the aisle next to theirs. She puffed out a frustrated breath. "Gin-Gin. You scared us."

"Boo," Gin said. "Are you guys talking about ghosts? Do we have one? Can I hug him?"

"There's no ghost," Holly said. *At least not here.* But there might be one somewhere, and she was probably rattling a locked attic door, hoping to escape.

"Time to go, kids!" Daddy called out.

Holly closed the book in her hands and slid it into her backpack while Jordan picked up the titles from the floor.

"Don't you have to tell your dad if you're taking a book home? What if someone wants to buy it tomorrow and he can't find it?" he asked.

"I'll bring it back." *After* she was done with it. She hefted her backpack onto her back. She had important research to do tonight.

Rosie's Inn—that was what everyone in town called the pink three-story house on the corner of Kendall Street. But to Jordan, it would always be his oma's house: a second home that smelled like orange wood cleaner and fresh-baked cookies.

When Mom worked late at the diner, he usually came here for dinner, since Dad didn't seem to want him around.

He was learning a lot about being an innkeeper: how to prepare the rooms for guests and even how to take reservations over the phone. He glanced at the phone attached to the kitchen wall, almost hoping it would ring so he could practice.

The inn was empty, since the last guest checked out an hour ago. Good thing, too, because that guy smelled like a skunk.

Jordan couldn't imagine how he got sprayed. Unless he thought it was a cat and tried to pet it. No local would make that mistake. They knew not to startle the little stink bombers.

Oma was upstairs trying to clear the smell from the room by opening the windows and wiping everything down.

The oven timer beeped, and Jordan shoved his hands into oven mitts so he could pull the last tray of cookies from the oven. The sweet smell of oatmeal raisin cookies filled the kitchen, making his mouth water.

He wanted to eat one now, but Oma said if he waited until after dinner, he could have two. One now or two later . . .

It was a hard choice.

The hallway floor creaked as someone walked across the old floorboards, and Jordan looked over at the doorway. "Oma, why do I have to wait to have two cookies?"

She didn't answer.

The creaks and groans moved down the hallway toward the den, but . . . why couldn't he hear any footsteps? Oma wore soft shoes, but they still made a sound.

Curious, he shuffled to the doorway and peered out.

"Oma?"

There was no one in either direction. That didn't make sense. He heard *someone*.

The words from Holly's book tickled the back of his brain: *Ghosts are rumored to haunt places where they lived, died, or were buried.*

His eyes lifted to the collage of photographs covering the wall and found the picture of Opa. He lived here with Oma for a long time before he had a heart attack. In the den. The direction the creaks and groans had gone.

But what if it wasn't Opa? The book did say that sometimes ghosts haunted people. What if Mr. Berkshire *did* have a ghost and it followed Jordan here?

Fear made him cold all over.

He needed to talk to Holly. She would know what to do. And if she didn't, maybe her book would know.

He ducked back into the kitchen, stripped off the oven mitts, and grabbed the phone from the wall to call the Cross family.

The line rang and rang until someone finally picked up on the other end. "Cross family," Holly announced, trying to sound grown-up.

"Holly, we've got ghosts at the inn," Jordan blurted.

"Jordan? Did you say there's—"

Her voice disappeared, and her dad's voice said in the background, "What did I tell you about answering the phone, young lady?"

"Not to do it?" Holly asked.

"Exactly. Go help your mother with dinner." Mr. Cris's voice grew louder as he put the phone to his ear. "Jordan, is everything all right?"

"Yeah, but I really need to talk to Holly."

"It's getting late. You can talk to her tomorrow."

"But it's important."

Mr. Cris paused. "Are you at home alone?"

"No, I'm still at Oma's."

"Good. If you need help with something, I have no doubt your grandmother will help you. If she *can't* help you with whatever it is, I can come over after dinner."

"Could you bring Holly with you?"

Mr. Cris sighed. "No. She has bath time after dinner and then bedtime. If you need me after you talk to your grandmother, you can call me back."

"But—"

"Good night, Jordan."

Mr. Cris must've hung up, because the phone let out a high-pitched tone in his ear. Something thumped to the floor in the den, and Jordan peered around the door frame as he hung up the phone. Was the ghost throwing things?

This is bad. Very, very bad.

25

Holly cracked open the oven door to sniff the bubbling pizza while Mom chopped up lettuce for a salad. Holly didn't like salad. Too many yuckables.

But the pizza, with pineapple and pepperoni, smelled so good, she wanted to eat it all by herself.

Except her belly would only stretch so far before it popped like a birthday party balloon, so she would have to share. But she would make sure she got the piece with the most pineapple.

"Close the oven door, sweetheart. You're letting out the heat, and the pizza's still baking," Mom said.

Holly closed the door. "I wish Jordan could have pizza with us. He said he's having toast at the inn, and that sounds boring."

"I've always liked breakfast for dinner."

Pancakes were good. Even cheesy scrambled eggs. But toast needed lots of peanut butter and strawberry jam for Holly to eat it.

"Come help me with the salad," Mom said.

Holly climbed up onto the step stool in front of the counter. "What can I do?"

"You can cut up the baby carrots."

Mom placed a cutting board on the counter, a knife, and a bag of baby carrots. Holly's nose crinkled. Carrots were a sweet vegetable, like they were trying to trick her tongue into believing they were a treat, but she wasn't fooled. Little orange liars. They were as bad as lemons. Those didn't even taste like fruit. They tasted the way floor cleaner smelled.

"That's a big knife, so use it slowly and carefully," Mom said.

Holly rolled her eyes. "I'm not a baby, Mom. I can use a knife." She placed a carrot on the board, holding onto it, and then pushed the knife down on one end. The butt of the carrot shot off the cutting board like a rock from a slingshot and bounced across the kitchen floor.

Holly's mouth opened in surprise. That wasn't supposed to happen.

She chopped another piece, and it sprang off the cutting board, too, bouncing and rolling away. She'd heard of jumping *beans* but not jumping *carrots*.

She looked up at Mom. "There's something wrong with these carrots."

Mom laughed. "There's nothing wrong with the carrots. But there's a certain way to cut them. I'll show you."

Mom stepped behind her and reached around to take the knife, the end of her long braid tickling Holly's cheek. Holly tipped her head back to look up at her.

"Mom, am I gonna look like you when I get old?"

"Thirty-one is not that old, but yes, I think you'll look a lot like me."

"Will I get nose freckles too?" Daddy always kissed Mom's nose freckles because he said they were too cute and unique to pass up. Holly wanted some unique nose freckles.

Maybe then that mean fifth grader wouldn't call her Casper because her face was so white. It was mean to make fun of people for their skin color, but he did it anyway. It wasn't *her* fault God forgot to give her freckles.

"Most of my freckles came later," Mom said. "My mom, your granny, said they were sunshine kisses, and if you're out in the sunshine enough, you'll probably get some too."

Sunshine kisses. Holly liked that.

"How much later is *later?*" she wondered aloud.

"A few years."

Years? That may as well be her whole life. Maybe she could give herself some freckles instead of waiting for the sun to do it.

"Now watch how I cut the carrots." Mom grabbed the carrot with one hand and held the knife with the other. "Gentle pressure from one side of the carrot to the other."

Daddy swooped into the room, making airplane noises, as he held Gin above his head. She had her arms spread wide, giggling as she flew around the room.

"Ladies and gentlemen, we're about to hit some rough weather," Daddy announced. "Buckle your seat belts!"

Daddy wobbled, and Gin squealed as she bobbed up and down and side to side.

"Oh no! You're gonna crash!" Holly shouted, no longer interested in the carrots Mom was showing her how to chop.

Daddy swerved toward the refrigerator. "We're in for a rough landing! Brace yourselves!" He turned at the last second and scooped Gin up as high as he could before dropping her feetfirst to the floor. Her toes touched four times before she finally landed.

Gin laughed and twirled in a circle. "We made it!" She grinned up at Daddy. "Can we go again?"

Daddy rubbed his lower back like it was sore and smiled. "Maybe tomorrow, Gingersnap. You and your sister should go set the table for dinner."

"That's better than chopping carrots." Holly ducked under Mom's arm and grabbed Gin's hand, pulling her along through the door into the dining room. She dragged a chair over in front of the wooden hutch and climbed up. "I bet it would be cool to fly for real."

"With big white wings. Like angels."

Holly opened the glass doors and pulled out four plates. "I don't wanna be an angel. Angels have to be good all the time. I'd rather be a dragon."

She would be the kind of dragon that carried knights into battle, and she would breathe fire across the ground to scare away the enemy.

"I wanna be Surprise Pegasus," Gin said, pulling the cloth mats from one of the hutch's drawers. "From

29

My Little Pony. She laughs a lot like me, and we both like balloons."

Holly waited for Gin to lay the place mats and then put the plates on them. "If you were a Pegasus, you could fly up and get the cookies Mommy puts on the top shelf. And then we could eat them under the blankets in bed at night."

Gin grinned. "We could have *all* the cookies."

"Don't forget the silverware, Gin-Gin."

"But it's pizza."

"And salad."

"Ohhh," Gin said, drawing out the word in a whine as she stomped her foot. "I don't like salad."

"You're only saying that 'cause I hate salad. You always eat yours."

"Well, that's 'cause . . . carrots are sweet and . . . I like the crunch lettuce makes. Oma lets me eat it straight from the garden. But . . . I wanna be like you, so . . . I don't like salad anymore."

"Mom says she couldn't handle two of me. That means you have to be you."

Gin sighed. "Okay. If I have to." Hanging her head, she shuffled through the door into the kitchen to get silverware.

Holly added bowls and glasses to the table before closing the doors of the china hutch. Her reflection stared back at her from the glass doors—all shallow and distorted because it wasn't a whole person.

30

Was that what ghosts were like?

Shallow-reflection people who weren't whole enough to walk around like living people anymore?

If she could do some reading tonight, she would find out for sure. She would wait until after Mom tucked them in, and then she would hide under her blanket with a flashlight so she could stay up late reading.

She'd done that before, and even when Daddy peeked in to check that they were asleep, he could never tell she was gobbling up stories under her blanket.

"What do I do?" Jordan asked himself.

He was on his own to deal with this situation, and that was almost scarier than the ghost itself. Holly was always his backup when he was facing something bad— bullies, trees with faces that might eat people, snarling dogs with huge teeth.

She would've marched down the hall to investigate by now, because she was brave like that, but he was still standing in the kitchen doorway.

"I can be brave."

He didn't have a protective suit like they did in *Ghostbusters*, so he grabbed the only thing he did have: the oversized oven mitts he'd dropped on the floor. He tugged them on to protect his hands, blew out a breath, and inched toward the den in his socks. Every step forward made him want to scurry back in the other direction.

"Don't be a chicken," he whispered.

If he managed to sneak up on a ghost, Holly would think he was the coolest person ever. Even Dad would be impressed, *if* he could prove he'd done it.

The tinkle and growl of piano keys from up ahead made him rub at his ears. Jordan wasn't a piano player, but even he knew those notes sounded like nails on a chalkboard when played together. Whoever this ghost was, he wasn't a musician.

Keeping his feet in the hallway, Jordan peeked around the door frame into the den. The cover for the piano keys was up, and a cup lay on the floor beside Opa's reading chair, but he didn't see anyone.

"H-hello?"

He half expected something to come flying at his face, but nothing happened. A clang came from his left, and Jordan whirled toward the fireplace. The fire poker swayed in its holder, clanking against the other tools.

"What . . ."

And then he saw a furry monster sitting on the stones in front of the fireplace, fur covered in gray ash like he'd rolled through the leftovers of last night's fire, and head wrapped in layers of spiderwebs.

Jordan sagged against the door frame, relieved and a little disappointed to find that his ghost was a cat. A really dirty one that must've been crawling through places that hadn't been cleaned in years.

"How did you get in here?"

Oma didn't have any pets.

"Did you find my cat burglar?"

Jordan jumped at the sound of Oma's voice echoing down the hall, still on edge after the whole ghost scare. She was at the bottom of the staircase toward the front of the house.

"He snuck in while I was gardening this morning," she said, walking down the hall to join him. "And I've been looking all over for him."

"Where'd he come from?"

"Considering how skinny he is, I expect he's a stray." She came up beside him, arms full of the skunky, wadded-up sheets and blankets. Crinkles formed around her eyes as she smiled. "Oh my. Look at him covered in all that ash. He's like a feline Cinderella."

"Cinderella was a girl."

"You're right. I suppose he's more of a ... Cinder*fella*."

"Are you gonna keep him?"

"Oh, I don't know, Jordy. Taking care of an animal is a large responsibility and not one anyone should take lightly."

"But he's not getting enough food out there. A home would be good for him, and he could hunt the mice that sneak into the storm cellar. And Opa was the only one allergic to animals. With him gone . . . I mean, since he's not here . . . you could have a pet."

Oma was quiet for a moment, her eyes a little sad. "Your poor grandfather was so allergic to pet dander, his eyes would swell shut."

"Do you think Opa might ever come back to visit us?"

Oma tipped her head at the question. "He's in heaven, liebling. We'll see him again someday but not here on this earth."

Jordan almost wished ghosts were real, like Holly thought they were, because then he could see and talk to Opa now instead of waiting until heaven. And that might make Oma happy too. She told his mom once that a part of her died with Opa . . . which didn't make sense. She wasn't a zombie. It probably meant she missed him a lot.

"It's strange to think I almost cheated myself out of a life with your grandfather. What a mistake that would've been," she said.

"What do you mean?"

"When I was young, I was in love with the idea of being in love, but I wasn't having much luck here in the United States, so I was seriously considering moving back to Germany where I still had family."

Young?

Jordan tried to imagine Oma as a *not* old person, but it wouldn't work. In his head, she always had gray hair and wrinkles, and she was always married to Opa.

"I wanted to be married. To know that when I came home, the man I loved would always be there. I wanted a partner I could laugh with and grow old with. Someone—"

"You're not gonna start talking about gross stuff, are you?" Jordan asked. He would rather scoop dirt with potato chips and eat them than hear about a bunch of smoochy old people.

Oma's eyebrows lifted. "Gross stuff?"

"You know. Kissing and hand-holding."

"Oh yes, kisses and hand-holding. Terribly disgusting," she teased. "It's normal for a boy your age to think that, but someday you'll enjoy those things."

Jordan crossed his arms. "No, I won't. Boys don't like that kind of stuff."

"If you say so."

He *did* say so, and she wasn't going to change his mind.

"As I was saying before the kiss police interrupted, I wanted a husband. But I got impatient, and I almost moved away. But then . . . I got this feeling that I was supposed to wait. So I waited and waited, for almost a year, and then your grandfather walked into the shop where I was mending clothes."

"What was he like?"

"He looked quite a bit like you." She ran a hand through Jordan's hair. "Blond hair, blue eyes, warm smile. But he had an adventurous spirit. He wanted to see and

35

experience everything. It took marrying him and opening this inn to force him to put down roots."

Jordan perked up at her answer. "Marrying him made him stay here with you?"

"It gave him a reason to settle in and build a life. He learned that sometimes the best things are right in front of you. You don't have to go looking for them elsewhere. And I learned that, even though we want something very much, if we're willing to wait on God's timing instead of rushing into things, He will bring something . . . or someone . . . wonderful into our lives. And after all the waiting, we will appreciate that person even more."

Jordan thought about that. "Like how I waited years for a friend?"

"That's a good example. I remember when you came to talk to me about some older boys who promised to be your friends, but they wanted you to do bad things to earn that friendship."

They wanted him to set off firecrackers at school and steal candy from the local store for them. Even though doing those things would've gotten him in trouble, he wanted a friend badly enough that he thought about doing them.

"After we talked, you decided to wait for a real friend. Someone who wanted to spend time with you just because. And then you met Holly a few months later."

Holly was his best friend. She liked to go on adventures and play ball with him, and even if she teased him about being a scaredy-cat sometimes, she always made him feel important. Gin was his friend, too, but she was a girly girl who wanted to play dress-up and Barbies, and he was not going to play with dolls.

"What do you think?" Oma asked. "Was Holly a friend worth waiting for?"

Jordan looked at the floor and shrugged, feeling a little embarrassed. "Yeah, I guess so."

"You guess so." Oma laughed softly. "You two couldn't be more attached at the hip if you were Siamese twins."

"I just wish God didn't wait so long sometimes. It was hard not having friends."

"I know, liebling. Some moments of waiting are longer than others. That's why we practice patience. The more you practice something, the easier it becomes."

"Is that why I have to wait until after dinner for my two cookies? Because you want me to practice patience?"

She laughed again. "I should say yes because it would make me sound clever, but no. I said that because I don't want you to spoil your dinner by filling up on cookies."

Man, if he'd known that, he could've eaten them when they were gooey and warm.

"I know we have a guest coming tonight, and I'm supposed to let guests pick which cookies they want first, but can I save the last two chocolate chunk cookies for Holly and Gin? We're going back to help Mr. Berkshire tomorrow, and I want to bring snacks."

"What's wrong with taking oatmeal raisin?"

Nothing, in his opinion. Oatmeal raisin cookies were some of the best, but Holly didn't think so. "Holly doesn't like raisins. She says they pretend to be chocolate chips in cookies, but then they turn out to be chewy rabbit poop."

Oma smiled. "That girl has such a colorful way of stating things. But she's wrong about the raisins. They're good, and they're good for you."

"I know." Holly was wrong about a lot, but she never liked to listen when he told her so. She only got more determined. "So can I save them for my friends?"

"Yes, you may save them for your friends." She looked back at the cat by the fireplace and sighed. "I suppose we can open the inn to this little one. But only if you can tame him and clean him up."

The cat extended his claws as he spread his toes to clean between them, all while giving Jordan the evil eye. *Come try it, and I'll shred you like cheese*, his eyes said.

Jordan rubbed his oven-mitted hands together. "Uh, I'm not sure I can do that."

"I have faith in you. Catch him before he gets ash on the furniture. He's going to need a bath." She left him alone with the wild cat.

Jordan crouched in the doorway and held out one of his oven-mitt-covered hands. "Come here, kitty. Come here, Cinderfella."

The cat hissed at him.

Jordan dropped his hand. He was going to need thicker oven mitts, a fishing net, and some shredded chicken from the icebox.

Poke. A bug stung Holly's bare arm, and she woke up just enough from her sleep to swat at it. She must've missed because it came right back.

Poke, poke.

"Holly," the bug whispered, so close to her face that it tickled the inside of her ear. Why did the bug sound like her sister? "Are you awake?"

Holly cracked open one eyelid to see Gin standing beside her bed, then snapped it shut with a muttered "No."

"That's a fib. I saw your eyeball."

Holly groaned and dragged the blanket up over her head, rolling to face the wall. "It's too early, Gin-Gin. Go back to bed."

"I can't. I had a bad dream."

Gin's bad dreams were never actually scary. Once, she dreamed that a fox with a red balloon followed her around singing the Lamb Chop song.

This is the song that never ends . . .

Gin poked her shoulder. "It was really scary, Holly. I was a fish, and I was playing jump rope in a garden, and this bunny tried to eat me. He bit my fin. See?"

Holly puffed out a breath and flung the blanket away from her face to find Gin pointing at her forearm. "It was a dream, Gin-Gin. There's no bite on your arm."

"Are you sure? I can still feel his big teeth. I think I need a Band-Aid."

"You don't need a Band-Aid."

"But I do. That was the meanest bunny I've ever met in my whole life, and he almost chewed me to bits."

Holly scooted upright in bed, pushing aside the book she stayed up way too late reading last night. Except for a few flashes of faraway lightning, barely any light peeped through the curtains. Even the sun thought it was too early to be awake. "You should stop watching *Bugs Bunny* before bed."

"Why? He's not mean. He's a funny bunny."

"That chews carrots to bits."

"But I wasn't a carrot."

You weren't a fish either, Holly wanted to say, but she was too tired to argue. All she wanted to do was go back to sleep, but that wasn't going to happen until Gin went back to sleep. "If you need a Band-Aid, go to the bathroom and get one."

Gin sucked in a breath, eyes wide. "But the hallway is scary at night, and the shadow bogeys will get me."

Holly knew all about the shadow bogeys. She used to be afraid of them, too, afraid they might reach out of the darkness and grab a toe that wasn't under the blanket or snap at her ankles in the hallway like piranhas.

But she wasn't scared anymore. Mostly.

She pushed away her blanket. "I'll get you a Band-Aid, but then you have to go back to sleep."

"I will."

"Promise?"

"Cross my heart, and my toes, tickle my chin, and tap my nose," Gin said, going through each motion.

Holly sighed and slid out of bed, opening the bedroom door to peek out. There was a flickering nightlight plugged in to one of the outlets, but the long hallway was as dark and spooky as the bowels of a pirate ship.

The floorboards creaked and shifted, and mysterious shadows danced on the walls. It was even worse when it was storming, like it was now, because raindrops slapped against the windows like waves that might drag the ship down into the murky depths of the ocean.

Holly glanced at Freckles, her stuffed bunny, on the dresser. She was getting too old to carry around her favorite stuffed animal, but he made her feel safer. She could be a big girl tomorrow. Tonight she needed Freckles.

She grabbed her stuffed bunny and tucked him under one arm.

"Watch out for bogeys," Gin whispered.

"I will." With a deep breath, Holly stepped into the hall.

Some of the boards squeaked and dipped beneath her bare feet, and flashes of lightning outside made the shadows dance and flicker on the walls.

She squeezed Freckles tighter and walked fast.

The bathroom was all the way at the other end of the hall. Right next to the old paint-chipped door that led to the attic.

What if our attic is haunted like Mr. Berkshire's?

Her book didn't say anything specific about attics, but with what Timmy and Mr. Berkshire said about theirs, she couldn't help but wonder. She'd never been up there. Daddy said the floor wasn't finished, and it was too dangerous for her and Gin.

She'd heard strange noises coming from up there before, but Daddy said it was only the house shifting as it got older.

As she passed the paint-chipped door, a draft crept out from beneath it and whispered across her bare toes, making her shiver.

Ghost breath.

She scampered into the bathroom to grab a Band-Aid and then raced back down the hall to the bedroom, closing the door behind her. She leaned against the door, breathing hard. She'd made it.

"You're back!" Gin said, shifting onto her knees on Holly's bed. "Did you get me a Band-Aid?"

Holly lifted her hand with the Band-Aid, but it wasn't there. Where did it go? She bent to look at the bedroom floor, lifting one foot and then the other. It wasn't there.

Oh Poohsticks.

She must've dropped it in the hallway. She opened the door and poked her head out, searching the spooky shadows. She spotted it near the flickering nightlight, but it was too far away to lean over and grab.

She would have to go out and get it, but she didn't feel brave enough to do that again. Not with the ghost breath coming from the attic.

An idea popped into her head.

"Gin, where's your sticky foot?"

"Mr. Wiggles is in his egg. I'll get him." Gin climbed out of bed to get her plastic egg and brought it over.

Holly snapped it open and pulled out the sticky foot. It was stretchy, which made it perfect for flinging and sticking to walls and ceilings. And hopefully, Band-Aids.

Tongue poking into her cheek, Holly flung the sticky foot. It landed a couple inches in front of the Band-Aid. She pulled it back to try again. It splattered against the nightlight the second time. The fifth time, it landed on the Band-Aid and sent it sliding close enough to grab.

"Yes!" Holly whisper-cheered. She closed the door and handed the sticky foot back to her sister.

Gin folded it back into the egg and then petted the shell. "Good job, Mr. Wiggles."

"Here's your Band-Aid."

Gin pointed to a spot on her arm. "Can you put it on? Right there."

Holly placed the bandage over the spot. "All better. Time to go back to sleep like you promised."

"Can I cuddle with you in your bed?"

"Yeah."

Gin hopped into the bed and wriggled beneath the blanket. Holly started to climb into bed with her when she noticed someone in the backyard. She lowered her foot back to the floor and walked to the window, opening one of the curtains.

A man stood by the trees—tall with dark hair and a gray raincoat that didn't cover his head. Too tall to be a

45

normal person. He looked up at her, and she gasped, ducking away from the window.

"What is it?" Gin asked. "Did you see a fairy? I wanna see."

Holly shook her head. "Not a fairy." That giant would scare the wings off fairies and send them all tumbling from the sky.

Gin scooted off the bed to come look. She turned her head left and right. "I don't see anything."

How could she not see the giant in the backyard? He was so big, he could use tree branches for toothpicks. "He's by the trees."

Gin squinted and pressed her face close to the glass. "I still don't see him."

Holly leaned over far enough to peek through the edge of the window and frowned in confusion. Gin was right. He wasn't there. He couldn't have run away that fast, could he?

"Do you think he went invisible?" Gin asked.

"Maybe."

But there was only one spooky being that could go invisible, and it wasn't giants, goblins, or ghouls. Holly turned her gaze to the book on her bed, the pages still open to the chapter about ghosts.

Interesting.

Jordan yawned as he shuffled into the kitchen, drawn from his room by the crackle of bacon in a skillet.

Mom was making breakfast.

His legs always felt extra heavy in the morning, like someone had filled them with rocks while he slept, and he dropped into one of the kitchen chairs hard enough to make the legs squeak across the floor.

Mom, standing in front of the stove, turned to look at him. "Morning, baby. Your cat scratches look better today."

Jordan touched the scratch on his forehead. Cinderfella had gotten him good, and more than once. Oma practically bathed him in peroxide before Mom picked him up last night. "I'm not sure that cat can be tamed. He's mean."

"He was most likely scared because he's not used to people. He'll get used to you in time."

"What if he doesn't? Oma won't let him stay if he's means to people, and if we put him back outside, he might starve." And he didn't want to see that happen.

"If he really can't be tamed, we'll take him to Ms. Emily. She'll know what to do with him. She might even know a barn with a high mice population. He would be happy and well fed there."

Ms. Emily was Holly and Gin's mom, and she was the town veterinarian. She took care of almost everyone's animals. Holly wanted to work with her someday, but

Jordan wished Holly would do that *without* traveling the world first.

"Mom, did you know Opa was a traveler?"

Mom cracked an egg into a bowl. "I don't remember him doing much traveling, but I do remember he was always reading *National Geographic* and talking about amazing places around the world he wanted me to see."

"Oma said once they got married, he stopped. He stayed here in Stony Brooke."

"Apart from driving to work at a factory a few towns over, that's true." She whisked the eggs in the bowl, scrambling them up. "He spent most of his time with me and Mom."

Jordan curled and uncurled his toes on the tile floor as he worked up the nerve to ask his next question. "Do you think, um, could I . . . could I marry Holly?"

Mom stopped whipping the eggs. "I expected this conversation someday, but not for at least another nine years."

"She said she wants to explore the world, but I don't want her to go. She's my best friend, and if she leaves, I might never see her again."

"Marriage isn't going to fix that, honey."

"Yes, it will. You used to say you married your best friend, and now you're always together. You get to hang out and eat together all the time, and that would be cool."

Mom smiled. "There's a bit more to marriage than that, and it's a grown-up decision. A union between two adults in love with each other. You're ten, and Holly's nine. Why don't we save this discussion for when you're both over the age of eighteen?"

"But she could be gone by then."

"I don't think she's going anywhere. With the vet clinic and the bookstore, her family is very established here, and it wouldn't make sense for them to move."

"But she still might leave when she's older."

Mom set the bowl of eggs on the counter and came to sit in the chair across from him. "I know how long you waited for friends, honey, and you're afraid to lose them, but marriage isn't the answer. Even if the two of you get married someday, you can't stop her from exploring the world if it's a part of who she is."

Jordan released a sigh, disappointed.

"Don't worry. If Holly decides to leave Stony Brooke someday, something tells me she'll invite you to go along. You're as special to her as she is to you." She kissed his forehead and got up to finish breakfast.

Jordan hoped that was true. Holly usually invited him to go with her when she went on one of her adventures.

"I know you're planning to spend most of the day with the girls today, so get your chores done before you go," Mom suggested.

"Chores?" Jordan groaned and slouched in his chair. "Do I have to?"

Mom turned a hard stare on him. "Jordan Bartholomew, after everything your father and I do to pay for this house, provide your food and your clothes—which are always filthy and full of holes from your adventures—is that a serious question?"

Jordan shrank a little lower in his chair. "No. But we're gonna spend all morning cleaning Mr. Berkshire's house. Doesn't that count?"

"What you're doing for that old man is an act of kindness. It doesn't replace your chores. Take out the trash and straighten up your room before you go. It looks like a tornado ripped through it."

Jordan folded his arms. "It's fine. I know where everything is."

Mom's eyebrows went up her forehead into the danger zone. *Uh oh.* He probably shouldn't have said that thing about his messy room being fine.

"I'll clean it," he said quickly. "Please don't take my Nintendo." He would go crazy if he couldn't play his games before bed.

"You better." She poured the whipped eggs into a skillet. "Now, do me a favor and go get your father. Breakfast is almost ready."

"Where is he?"

"Outside, straightening up the garage."

Jordan pushed up from his chair and slipped out the back door. Dad had been talking about organizing the garage for months. "Dad?"

Dad was wearing jeans and a T-shirt today instead of his sheriff's uniform, since he was off on the weekends. He glanced at Jordan as he lifted a box onto the metal shelf by the wall. "What is it, Jordan?"

"Mom said breakfast is ready." He noticed his baseball glove and ball on top of one of the boxes. "Hey, Dad, since you're off work today, do you think we could play catch?"

Dad stacked another box. "I've got things to do today."

"I know, but maybe just . . . for a few minutes? We can set a timer so you don't miss the other stuff you have to do. I've gotten really good at my fastball, and I wanted to show you."

"Not today."

Jordan's hopes sank. "What if I help you clean the garage so you have more time?"

"You can't even clean your own bedroom, and you want to help me clean the garage?" Dad shook his head. "I want things done a certain way, so I'd rather do it myself."

"But I—"

"I said no, Jordan, and that's the end of it," Dad cut in, his voice quiet but firm.

Jordan's chin quivered, and he tried to blink away his tears before they could fall.

Dad set an old radio on the shelf. "Don't start with that. What have I told you about the sniffling and tears?"

"That real men don't cry."

"That's right, so wipe your face, straighten your shoulders, and go inside. Tell your mother I'll be there in a minute."

"Yes, sir." Jordan hung his head and shuffled back inside, doing his best to hide his tears.

After seeing the disappearing ghost in the raincoat, Holly couldn't go back to sleep. Her head was too full of thoughts, and they fluttered around like a bird in a cage.

Who was he? He must have a name and a story. An interesting one, most likely.

Why was he standing at the edge of her backyard? Her book said ghosts haunted places important to them. What was so important about her yard?

Could he be related to Goliath? He was awful big to be a normal person. He could probably squash a normal person with his giant feet.

Why had she never noticed him before?

Why did he disappear after she *did* notice him? Was he shy or sneaky?

Why was he wearing a raincoat? Could ghosts feel raindrops? Maybe the raincoat was what he was wearing when he was last alive, and he would have to wear it forever, even if it was sunny and hot.

How long was forever?

Holly thought about all the questions as she sat in front of her bedroom mirror, stuffed bunny in her lap, and tapped dots onto her nose with a washable brown marker.

She wanted to look more like Mom, with pink cheeks and little nose freckles. The only time Holly had freckles was when she went splashing through mud puddles, and mud freckles didn't count.

She tapped a few more freckles across her cheeks, then tilted her face in every direction to study them. "Perfect."

Gin plopped down beside her in her blue butterfly dress. "Can I have polka dots too? Blue ones?"

"They're not polka dots. They're freckles like Mom's, so they can't be blue."

"Oh. Okay." Gin closed her eyes and pushed her face forward, waiting.

Quirking her lips to one side, Holly tried to decide where would be the best place for her sister's freckles. She added a dozen dots in different sizes, but Gin giggled on the last one, and the tip of the marker slid across her cheek, leaving a brown line.

"Gin, you have to stay still."

Gin puckered her lips inward and tried not to move them as she whispered, "Sorry. I won't move anymore."

Holly licked her thumb and rubbed away the brown line before adding one last dot. "All done."

Gin opened her eyes and gasped at her reflection. "Wow! Holly, we look like twins again!"

Holly grinned. They always looked like twins. Even with the different clothes they wore and the different hairstyles, they looked the same. Except Holly *might* be an inch taller. She would ask Daddy to measure her before breakfast.

Gin's stomach growled, and she patted it. "My belly gremlin's hungry."

Holly snapped the lid back on the marker and got to her feet, pulling Gin up alongside her. "Let's go get breakfast."

She glanced at the attic door as they left the bedroom, but there was nothing scary about it during the day. Even the hallway was all back to normal.

She started down the steps, Gin hopping along and humming behind her.

Mom's voice carried up from the kitchen. "When Miriam called this morning, she said she saw a man wandering around in the woods during her walk. She's all worked up over it."

Daddy grunted. "It was probably Mr. Peterson. He likes walking through nature and taking pictures of the wildlife. Mostly birds, I think."

Holly frowned as she tried to picture Mr. Peterson in her mind, but she couldn't.

"Peterson," Mom said. "Is he the guy we met at church a few months ago? Tall, dark hair, strong opinions about animal welfare?"

"One and the same."

That sounded like the man Holly had seen at the edge of the woods this morning, which meant her ghost wasn't even a ghost. He was a boring bird-watcher guy. *Rats.*

"I remember him," Mom said. "He asked if he could shadow me at the veterinary clinic to make sure the animals were being treated well. As if I would stand for any animal to be mistreated in my care."

Gin bounced into the kitchen ahead of Holly and twirled. "Look, Daddy! We have freckles like Mommy. Aren't we pretty now?"

Daddy scooped her up, propping her on his hip, and studied her face. "Pretty? My girls are more than pretty. They're *beautiful* exactly the way God made them. With"—he kissed one of Gin's marker freckles—"or without freckles." He kissed her clear cheek, making her giggle.

"Even if we look like Casper?" Holly asked.

Daddy frowned. "Who said that to you?"

"A boy in town."

"What boy?"

"Colton."

"What's Colton's last name?"

"Cris, let me . . ." Mom looked over at Daddy, and he closed his mouth, his frown even bigger than before. Mom sat down in one of the kitchen chairs and held out her hands to Holly. "Come here, baby girl."

Holly shuffled over, placing her hands in her mom's.

"What that boy said hurt your feelings, didn't it?" Mom asked.

"No," Holly said, then, realizing it was a lie, looked at the floor and mumbled, "Maybe a little."

"Maybe a *lottle*?"

Holly looked up with a grin. "Mommy, that's not a word."

"I know. But it's okay to admit when something hurts your feelings a lot. Being able to express that with your words is important and healthy." She rubbed her thumbs over Holly's knuckles. "People will always have opinions, and some of them won't be very nice. But opinions are only their thoughts and feelings. They're not facts, and they're not even always true. What's important to remember is what God says about you. Do you know what He says?"

"That I'm frightfully made?"

Mom laughed. "*Fear*fully made. A lot of people think *fearfully* means scared, but in that Bible verse, it means 'with respect' and 'heart-felt interest.' God was so, so interested in who you would be. With His whole heart and His careful hands, God made you exactly the way He

57

wanted you. With your red hair, your fair skin, your big heart, and your kind nature, you are fearfully and wonderfully made, my little Holly. Always remember that."

Holly thought about that. "Since God made me the way I am, could I ask Him for a favor?"

"What kind of favor?"

"I wanna be tall like you and Daddy."

Mom smiled. "It could happen. You have a lot of growing to do."

"Or she could end up five feet tall like your mother," Daddy said. "Step stools for life. Only time will tell."

"I think I grew a lot last night," Holly said.

"Well, let's find out." Daddy set Gin down and grabbed the pencil from the counter.

Holly stepped up against the door frame, which was covered with lines marking their growth ever since they could stand. She straightened her back, standing as tall as possible, and waited for Daddy to draw the line.

"Did I grow?" She turned to see the line.

"A whole half inch."

She pumped her fist into the air. "Yes!"

"Me next!" Gin squeezed in and stood against the frame.

The phone rang, and Mom picked it up while Daddy measured Gin. She listened for a moment, then said, "All right. I need to stop by the clinic to get some supplies, and then I'll be right over." She hung up.

"You're not coming to Mr. Berkshire's?" Holly asked.

"I'm sorry, sweetie, I have to work."

"But Brandy's supposed to work on the weekend so you can be home. That's what you said."

"I know, but there's an emergency Brandy doesn't know how to handle. Ms. Katie's horse is having trouble giving birth, and I may need to help deliver the foal. Otherwise, he might not make it."

"Oh," Holly said, disappointed. But saving a baby horse was more important than scrubbing floors with them. "Can you take a picture of the baby?"

Mom patted her purse. "I have the camera right here. And I promise I'll be home before dinner, and then I want to hear all about your day."

Mom kissed the top of Holly's head, then Gin's, before hugging Daddy and kissing him good-bye too.

Daddy put away the measuring pencil. "What do you girls say we start this day with some pancakes?"

Gin hopped up and down. "I want princess castle pancakes! With blueberries and a maple syrup river."

Daddy's eyes narrowed in thought. "How about a moat?"

"What's a moat?"

"That's the water that goes around the castle," Holly explained. "Like a donut river."

59

Gin drew in a breath of amazement. "Daddy, can I have a blueberry maple moat?"

"Your wish is my command, Lady Ginevieve." Daddy bowed, and Gin squeaked with delight. "And what would you like, my little Jelly Bean?"

"Marshmallow chocolate chip."

"I should've known."

Holly smiled and plopped down at the table. Mornings that started out with Daddy's pancakes were the best mornings.

Jordan tossed his baseball into the air as he walked down the road toward Mr. Berkshire's house, catching it in his glove. He wished Dad would play catch with him, but he was always too busy.

"Not today, Jordan," he muttered, deepening his voice to mimic his dad. "*Never* is more like it."

He kicked a rock and watched it bounce down the road. Why couldn't he be as important as catching fish or cleaning the garage or watching sports on TV?

Why didn't Dad ever have time for *him*?

Jordan was willing to learn almost anything—how to fix a car, how to shoot a gun, even how to repair a bathroom sink. But Dad only wanted him out of the way, like he was some annoying fly buzzing around his head.

He swiped at a tear on his cheek and kicked another rock.

At least he had Holly. She would play catch with him. She wasn't very good at the catching or the throwing part, which was annoying sometimes, but at least she tried. That was more than Dad ever did.

He tossed the ball, but when he tried to catch it, it hit the edge of his glove and bounced out, rolling away.

He sighed and dropped his gloved hand to his side. "Stupid ball."

It rolled to a stop in front of the leaning fence surrounding Mr. Berkshire's yard.

Mr. Cris, who had just climbed out of his car with the twins, picked up the baseball and turned it over in his hands before looking at Jordan. "Hey, kiddo."

"Hey, Mr. Cris." Jordan swiped another tear from his cheek with his sleeve and sniffed. He didn't want anyone to know he'd been crying.

Holly's dad frowned and studied him, still holding the ball with both hands. "Girls, why don't you go inside and say good morning to Mr. Berkshire. Jordan and I will join you in a few minutes."

"Okay, Daddy!" Gin rushed over to hug Jordan first, trapping his arms at his sides. "Hi, Jordan. I love you."

He tried his best to pat her back. "Hi, Gin."

She smiled and released him, then skipped up the sidewalk to the house. Holly eyed Jordan curiously as she followed her sister, trying to figure out what was wrong.

Jordan shuffled forward. "Did I do something wrong, Mr. Cris?"

"Not to my knowledge." He tossed the ball back, and Jordan caught it with his mitt. He leaned onto the hood of his car and folded his arms. "You were doing okay last night when we dropped you off at your oma's. You want to tell me what's wrong?"

Jordan shrugged. "I wanted to play catch with Dad. I thought . . . since he didn't have to work today . . ."

"But he said no?"

Jordan stared at his feet as he nodded. "Yeah, but he's really busy and there's not a lot of time in the day."

"We all have the same amount of time in the day. How we choose to spend it and whom we choose to spend it with is important. *You* are important."

Jordan sniffled and looked up at him. "Then why doesn't he wanna spend time with me?"

Mr. Cris's eyes turned sad. "I don't know, buddy. What I do know is . . . he's missing out on one awesome kid. He's lucky to have you, whether he knows it or not."

"I don't know about that."

"That's okay, because I do."

Jordan wiped at the tears on his face. "Sorry for crying. I'm trying not to."

"It's okay to cry when your heart is hurting, Jordan."

"Dad says real men don't cry."

Mr. Cris let out a slow breath. "Come here for a minute."

Jordan shuffled over and sat on the hood of the car beside him, rolling the ball around in his glove.

"God gave all of us the ability to cry. Not just girls and women. All of us. And He did that because sometimes our emotions build and build inside us until there's too much pressure for us to hold—like too much water in a balloon. We need to let some out before we explode, and tears help us do that," Mr. Cris explained. "The most courageous and masculine man I've ever known, the *best* man I've ever known, cried. Do you know who that man is?"

"No." Jordan snagged another stray tear with his sleeve.

"Jesus."

"Jesus cried?"

"He did. The Bible says He wept."

"Why?"

"I think it was because He saw the pain his friends were in, and it made His heart hurt." Mr. Cris wrapped an arm around Jordan's shoulders. "Your dad may have been raised to believe men don't cry, but Jesus is our example. It's okay to be sad sometimes, and it's okay to cry." He pulled Jordan into a side hug, giving him a squeeze. "Now, what do you say we toss that ball around a little bit before we go in?"

Jordan looked at the ball in his mitt. "We don't have to."

"Baseball is never about *having* to. It's about wanting to because it's fun. Don't get me wrong, I love my girls, and I wouldn't trade them for the world, but they would rather chase butterflies than play sports, and sometimes a guy needs another guy to toss a ball around with."

Jordan smiled. "I've seen them do that."

Mr. Cris stood and stepped away from the car, raising his hands. "Head back over there and let's see what you've got."

"But you don't have a glove."

"I'll be all right." He punched a fist into his open palm. "Mitts of steel. Give me your best."

Excitement pushed through the sadness Jordan had been feeling all morning. He hopped up and sprinted back to where he'd been standing before. He drew back his arm and flung the ball.

Mr. Cris caught it and whistled. "That was a nice one." He tossed it back, and Jordan grabbed it with his glove. "Put a little speed behind the next one."

Jordan did, and Mr. Cris shook the sting from his hand after he caught. "Do me a favor. Try to avoid my windshield with that glass-shattering fastball."

Jordan grinned. "Yes, sir." He snagged the return throw from the air, his sadness draining away with each toss and catch of the ball.

Mr. Berkshire's front door was open, but he was nowhere in sight. Gin went searching for him, peeking behind curtains and inside closets like they were playing hide-and-seek.

Holly smeared some of the dirt from the front window with her sleeve and watched as Daddy and Jordan tossed the baseball around.

Her best friend was sad, and that made *her* feel sad. She would bet every marshmallow in her snack bag that Jordan's dad was the reason. He was almost always the reason. Sheriff Radcliffe might keep everyone in town safe from bad stuff, but he was a booger. She would tell him so to his face if she wouldn't get in trouble for being rude to a grown-up.

"Mr. Berkenshire, where are you?" Gin called out in a singsong voice. She opened and closed the kitchen cupboards.

"It's *Berkshire*, Gin-Gin, not *Berken*shire, and he's too big to fit into the cabinets like we do."

"Oh." A cupboard door tapped shut, and Gin wandered around a bit more before going up the steps.

Holly could help her find old Mr. Berkshire, but she wanted to make sure Jordan was okay first. After a few more tosses of the ball, Daddy rested an arm on Jordan's shoulder, and they came up the sidewalk.

"There's a chance you could play professional baseball, if you put in the practice," Daddy said.

Jordan tossed the ball sideways into his glove. "I like football more. Maybe someday I'll be a running back."

"You've got the speed for it." Daddy stepped inside with Jordan behind him. He looked around the entryway. "Where's your sister?"

"She's playing hide-and-seek with Mr. Berkshire. Except Mr. Berkshire doesn't know he's playing. I heard her go upstairs."

"I'll find her. You two start cleaning the windows." Daddy left them alone by the front door.

Holly pulled the plastic bag from the pocket of her overalls and opened it, holding it out to Jordan. "Marshmallow?" They always made *her* feel better when she was sad.

"Nah, I'm good." Jordan leaned his ball and glove against the door where he wouldn't forget them when it was time to go. He gave her a funny look. "What happened to your face?"

Holly blinked at him, confused.

"You're covered in dots."

Oh, the freckles! She'd forgotten all about them.

"Mom has freckles around her nose and on her cheeks. Daddy says they're unique, and I wanted some, too, so I made some. You don't like them?"

Jordan puckered his lips inward and looked at his shoes, shrugging one shoulder and then the other. "I like your face the way it usually is."

"Why?" Her face wasn't unique like Mom's.

"I don't know. Because . . ." He shrugged again. "I just do."

Holly noticed the scratch on Jordan's cheek and forehead. "What happened to *your* face? Did you get in a fight with a cardboard box again?"

Jordan lifted his head with a scowl. "No, and that only happened once."

They had been building their first cardboard fort, and he wasn't paying attention when he crawled inside. He ended up with a paper cut on his head from the edge of the cardboard.

"The scratches are from a stray cat," he said.

"You found a cat?"

"I thought it was a ghost walking around Oma's place . . . thanks to your creepy book, but it was only a cat. Because ghosts aren't real."

Holly had been a lot more certain about ghosts this morning, before she found out the spooky figure in her backyard was an ordinary man. But her book said they were real, and Mr. Berkshire said there were some in his attic. Plus, there was the one in the Bible, and Daddy said every word of the Bible was true, so . . .

The hairs on the back of Holly's neck stood up without warning, and a shiver swept through her. She gasped as she looked around. According to her book, that meant a ghost had floated by.

"I found Mr. *Berken*shire!" Gin called out, bouncing down the steps beside Daddy. "He was hiding in the attic, but he wasn't really hiding. He was sitting on a box. He's not very good at hide-and-seek."

The attic?

But he couldn't be in the attic because that would mean he unlocked the door, and if he unlocked the door . . .

Holly dashed up both staircases to the attic and stopped in the doorway, breathing hard. The door stood wide open, and Mr. Berkshire sat on a crumpled cardboard box, staring at an old hat, his tired dog snoring beside his feet.

Holly inched inside. "Mr. Berkshire?"

He turned his head toward her. "Which one are you?"

"Holly. Gin's wearing a dress. And I'm half an inch taller."

He nodded. "Of course. I should've noticed." He turned his attention back to the purple hat with a green feather.

Holly looked around the attic. It was filled with boxes and colorful items that reminded her of a circus, and cobwebs hung from the rafters and boxes like white Christmas garland, but there was no sign of any spooky spirits. Only a white sheet shaped like a person.

The ghosts must've escaped. That was what she felt downstairs by the front door. They had floated past her and out into the world.

Holly opened her mouth to ask about them, but then she saw the tear slipping down Mr. Berkshire's cheek. She stepped over the pair of high-heeled shoes she'd seen through the crack below the door and came to stand in front of him.

"Mr. Berkshire, what's wrong?"

"Your question yesterday got me thinking about what was up here. I even managed to find the key in the junk drawer."

Jordan poked his head into the attic, wide eyes searching for any spiders that might be hanging from the ceiling on webs.

Mr. Berkshire petted the velvet hat in his lap. "I thought coming up here might help me let go, but . . . I shouldn't have opened that door."

"Because of the ghosts?"

He stared at her, like he was having a hard time remembering what they talked about yesterday. "Because of Marigold."

"Who's Marigold?" Jordan asked.

"She was . . . my best friend. We were in a traveling festival together. Like a circus, but not quite as large a production. It was called the Festival Funanza. We had animals, performances, even popcorn. People loved it."

"Were you a lion tamer? Or a tightrope walker?" Holly asked.

"No, I was a juggler. I could juggle eleven balls at one time."

"Wow," Jordan and Holly said. That was a lot. Holly had tried apple juggling once, but she couldn't even keep two apples in the air.

"That's my costume over there." Mr. Berkshire pointed to the person-shaped sheet.

Curious, Holly pulled the sheet aside and peeked under it. There was a metal pole with a doll stomach and head on top—sort of like the ones for clothing displays at stores—and there was a yellow-and-tan long-sleeve shirt with brown shoelaces keeping the material together around the chest.

Holly's nose wrinkled. "They made you dress like a banana?"

"Anything to increase festival attendance."

"Where did you set it up?" Jordan asked.

"In the field closest to the town square, but I did most of my performing in the square. So did Marigold. Sometimes I painted portraits for extra money." Mr. Berkshire aimed a knobby finger at a large painting leaning against a stack of boxes, a white sheet lying on the floor in front of it. "That was my Marigold."

Holly and Jordan crowded around the painting for a closer look.

Marigold had long brown hair and a pretty white dress with a square silver locket around her neck. Her hand rested on the head of a black-and-pink pig the size of a dog. It had a collar on, but there was no visible name. It was probably Pork Chop. That's what Holly would name the pudgy pig.

"Her name was Marigold Miller, but most everyone knew her as the pig whisperer. She raised swine and taught them to do tricks, like jumping through rings. Kids loved it. She always dressed like a fancy lady during the performance, which seemed to amuse people even more. I had this hat made for one of her performances." Mr. Berkshire held up the hat in front of him at a slight angle, like he was picturing it on Marigold's head. "She threw it at me in anger on that last day."

Jordan sat down cross-legged in front of him. "Why was she angry?"

"She wanted to get married and start a family, but I wasn't ready. Our disagreement turned into a fight. She left me, left the festival. I kept thinking she would come back, but she didn't. I was too angry and hurt to go after her. But then, about a year later, I finally went looking for her, only to discover she'd married someone else."

Holly frowned. "But if she married someone else all those years ago, why does she haunt you? Can't you both . . . move on?"

"We were meant to be together, but I ruined everything for both of us. I lost the love of my life, and we both lost our best friend—each other."

Holly's stomach cramped at the thought of losing a best friend. What would she do if she had to live the rest of her life without hers?

"She was furious with me the day I said I wouldn't marry her, and I suspect she'll be furious with me to the grave and beyond," he said. "I don't blame her."

Mr. Berkshire set the hat on top of a box, and Holly noticed the plastic candy glued to the side of it for decoration. "Why is there a peppermint candy on it?"

"One of the things I remember about my Marigold . . ." Mr. Berkshire smiled a little. "She had a sweet tooth like no one else."

"I bet I know someone." Jordan threw a look Holly's way. "She always has candy or marshmallows with her."

"All the best people do," Mr. Berkshire said.
He released a breath. "I need to go downstairs. Being here, surrounded by things from our life . . . it hurts too much."

He stood, his body crackling like bubble wrap. "Come, Rubio."

The dog stretched and yawned before following him to the door.

"Mr. Berkshire," Holly called out, grabbing his attention. "I'm sorry you lost Marigold."

He looked between them. "You're young yet, but someday you'll have important decisions to make. Think long and hard before you make those decisions. You don't want to be haunted for the rest of your lives like me."

He left them alone in the attic.

"Poor Mr. Berkshire." Holly picked up the hat and walked to the old mirror in the corner, placing the hat on her head to see how it looked. "He doesn't deserve to be haunted forever because he made a mistake. He deserves to be happy again, and we're gonna help him."

"How?"

Holly spun toward him with the fancy hat on her head. "We're going ghost hunting."

How are we supposed to hunt a ghost?

Jordan trudged after Holly, tired from scrubbing windows and hauling trash from Mr. Berkshire's house all morning and afternoon. The last thing he felt like doing was walking all over Stony Brooke.

"Can't we go back to your house and play squirt guns or something?" he asked. "It's hot." He couldn't even find a puddle from this morning's rain to jump in. They were all dried up.

"Maybe after," Holly said, marching forward in the pirate hat she'd used as part of her Halloween costume two years ago, the wooden sword tucked into the belt she'd wrapped around her waist.

"After what?"

"After we find Marigold."

"I'm still not sure about this whole ghost thing."

"You heard Mr. Berkshire. He wouldn't lie."

"People lie all the time to my dad, saying they didn't do stuff even though they did, so you can't say that for sure." Jordan tripped over a loose shoelace and scowled. "And if ghosts are real, how come they're not all over, and why haven't I seen any?"

"Because they can go invisible."

"Then how are we gonna find one?"

Holly stopped and turned to face him, patting her purple backpack. "With my ghost-hunting kit. That's why I packed it."

"What's in it?"

"Lots of stuff." She unzipped her bag and reached inside, pulling something out. "I've got my magnifying glass to follow any clues she leaves behind. I don't know what kind of clues exactly. My book only said that if there are ghosts, there will be evidence."

"Like footprints or something?"

Holly shrugged. "I bet we'll know it when we see it." She pulled his slingshot from her bag and handed it to him. "I brought this in case you need a weapon too."

"I've been looking all over for this. Where did you find it?"

"Gin's toy box. She was using it as a leash thing for her Barbie horses."

Jordan rolled his eyes. *Gin*. She *would* find a way to use it to play with her dolls.

"I brought my hoodicky so I know when any ghosts are trying to sneak past me while invisible, like they did at the house."

"Your what?"

Holly dug around in her backpack. "It's a spinny thingy, and it's in here somewhere. Oma gave it to me last summer, and she called it a hoodicky."

Jordan slapped his forehead. "A *doo*hickey. It's like any small, weird object."

She pulled out a bright pinwheel, the shiny fan spinning in the breeze. "Yeah, this thingy."

"How does a pinwheel help us find a ghost?"

"When they float past us, the wheel spins."

"But it's spinning right now."

She sighed. "That's the wind."

Jordan stuck a finger in the pinwheel, stopping it from spinning, and then removed his finger and watched it pick up speed again. "If the wind makes it spin and ghosts make it spin, how do you know which one it is?"

Holly stared at the pinwheel, looking a little unsure. "I'll know. I read a book about ghosts, so I'm basically an expert." She stuffed the pinwheel back into her bag.

"What else is in there?"

"Skittles because Mr. Berkshire said she likes sweets. We'll use those to lure her into a trap, and then we'll throw the sheet over her so she can't get away."

Jordan scrunched his face. "A bedsheet?"

"Yep. A white one."

"Is that what your book says?"

"No, it doesn't say anything about sheets. But think about it. Every time you see a picture of a ghost, they're covered in a white sheet. That's because ghosts are tran . . . translu . . ." Her nose wrinkled as she tried to come up with the word. "They're not whole people, like they're kind of see-through, and they don't show up in pictures. The sheet makes them visible. And if you can throw a sheet over them for a picture, then you can throw a sheet over them to catch them."

Jordan supposed that sort of made sense. When Holly stuffed the Skittles back into the bag and pulled out a bag of Twinkies, he asked, "What are the Twinkies for?"

"Snacks. All adventures need snacks."

Finally something he agreed with.

"So where are we going hunting?" he asked.

Please don't say the cemetery.

"The cemetery," she answered.

Jordan groaned. He couldn't really explain why, but cemeteries gave him the creeps. Even thinking about walking between the gravestones made him shiver. "It's not a good idea for us to go there."

"If you don't believe in ghosts, then why are you scared of the cemetery?"

Jordan frowned. "I didn't say I was scared."

"You have goose bumps."

Jordan rubbed at his arms in annoyance. "The cemetery is a big place, and we could get lost. Plus, I don't think there's a good reason."

"When Mr. Berkshire unlocked the attic, he let Marigold out. She would go somewhere important to her. Like her grave. So that's where we're going, but you don't have to come. You can go back. I won't even call you a chicken. Cross my heart." She drew an invisible X over her chest.

Jordan glanced over his shoulder in the direction of her house, tempted to go back. But he couldn't leave her to finish this adventure by herself. "I probably shouldn't let you go alone. There could be a fresh hole dug for a grave, and what if you fall in? There'll be nobody there to get you out."

"That's true." Holly spun to face forward and started walking again.

"So what are we gonna do when we find Marigold?"

"Mr. Berkshire's my friend, and Marigold's not allowed to haunt him anymore. When we find her, I'll tell her so, and if she gets feisty . . ." Holly drew her wooden sword from her belt. "I'll poke her till she decides to be nice." She slid the sword back into her belt. "Come on, we're almost there."

"How do we find her grave?"

"We shouldn't have to. As long as she doesn't know we're there, and she doesn't know to go invisible, we should be able to see her."

They walked the rest of the way to the town cemetery and wandered between the graves and past a couple of people laying flowers. Jordan held a pebble in the band of his slingshot and looked around, hoping they wouldn't find anything.

If they *did* find something, he would never be able to sleep again. How could he when an invisible ghost might be hovering over his bed?

Holly grabbed his arm and pulled him to the ground behind a grave and whispered, "Found her."

Jordan's eyes blinked wide. "What? Where?"

Holly pointed and then opened her backpack to drag out the sheet. Jordan leaned to his left to see where Holly had pointed, and his mouth dropped open in surprise.

Like the painting in Mr. Berkshire's attic, a woman with long brown hair and white clothes stood with her back to them, her head bowed as she hovered by a grave.

Holly puckered her lips between her teeth as she crouch-walked through the grass, slow and sneaky so Marigold couldn't see her coming.

She didn't want her to disappear.

She'd never confronted a ghost before—never even seen one—but how hard could it be?

Holly glanced back at Jordan, but all she could see were one eye and some of his blond hair as he peeked around the gravestone. She'd given him the sheet and told him to follow her. Instead, he was hiding.

Scaredy-cat.

She slowly stood behind Marigold, drew her wooden sword from her belt, and poked her in the back like she was going to make her walk the plank. "Gotcha!"

Marigold whirled around fast, her white dress whipping at the air like it was alive and angry.

Holly scrambled back so it couldn't get her, but she kept her sword aimed high. "You need to stop haunting my friend, Mr. Berkshire!"

Marigold stepped away from the sword. "Who's Berkshire?"

What did she mean, "Who's Berkshire?" Was she trying to be tricky?

Holly squinted against the sunlight to see Marigold's face. Wait a minute . . . something wasn't right. She was wearing white, and she had dark brown hair, but she didn't look anything like the woman in the painting. "You're not Marigold."

"No." The woman placed her hands on her hips. "My name is Annabelle."

That explained why she wasn't see-through. She was a whole, living person. "Oh, sorry I poked you with my sword."

"As you should be."

Holly looked at the name on the gravestone the woman was standing near, but it didn't belong to Marigold. She sighed and put away her sword. Ghost hunting was a lot harder than she thought it would be.

Annabelle had eyebrows with points in the middle, like hairy mountains, and both of them dipped low over her eyes. "Do your parents know you're attacking people in the cemetery with weapons?"

Attacking? It was only a little poke, and her sword wasn't even sharp. Daddy wouldn't let her have a sharp one. She'd asked. "I said sorry."

"And sorry is supposed to make everything better?"

"Well, I would take it back if I could, but I can't, so all I can say is sorry."

"Are you here by yourself?" Annabelle demanded.

"No, I'm here with my best friend. He's hiding behind that gravestone over there." Holly pointed, and Jordan popped to his feet.

"I'm not hiding. I was . . . tying my shoe."

Holly rolled her eyes. *Fibber.* "We thought you were the ghost that's been bothering our friend, and that you might come visit your own grave. I was trying to catch you so I could talk to you."

"How old are you, six?"

Holly bristled. "No, I'm nine."

Annabelle bent down, hands on her knees. "You should leave the ghost catching to the professionals. Adults who know what they're doing."

Jordan's eyes went wide. "You think ghosts are actually real?"

"I know they are. Because I've seen one. My sister appeared to me a couple of days after . . . she passed. It was only a glance, but I saw her."

"Where was she?" Holly asked.

"Home. Ghosts have no interest in cemeteries. They want to be where their loved ones are. Where they had a life." She straightened and stared down at Holly. "Now, what are your parents' names? I'd like to speak with them."

Uh-oh.

"I'm not gonna tell you that, 'cause you'll tattle on me."

"I'll figure out who they are at church. There can't be that many redheads in town."

"But I said sorry twice *and* told you I would take it back if I could."

"Sorry isn't always good enough. I believe in strict discipline." She picked up her purse from the ground.

83

"And children shouldn't be running wild through town like you two."

Wild? It wasn't like they were stampeding around town, destroying stuff, like a whole pack of buffalo.

Annabelle walked away.

Holly glared after her. "She's one of those . . . *difficult* souls. That's what Mom calls the cranky people who come into the clinic. She's definitely gonna be a polter . . . polter . . . one of those mean ghosts that throws things."

"Poltergeist," Jordan said. "It's German."

Polter*geist*? Holly thought about it, then decided she didn't like it. Polter*ghost* sounded better. She plunked down in the grass and opened her bag to grab the Twinkies. She waited for Jordan to join her, then handed him one. "I'm gonna get time-out again tomorrow. For *months*."

"Maybe not. There are two churches in town. She might go to the wrong one."

"I hope so."

Jordan crammed the whole Twinkie into his mouth and asked around the globs of sugary goodness, "What do we do now?"

Holly rested her Twinkie on her knees, thinking. "Annabelle might be mean, but she's right. Marigold wouldn't come here."

"Where do you think she would go?"

84

"Maybe the town square where they used to do the festival? Or to the house where she lived with her husband. We should walk through the rest of town, and then we can go to her house."

"How do we find her house?"

That was a good question.

"We can check the phone book. It has addresses. And if it's not there, I bet Oma would know. She knows everything." Holly grabbed the sheet Jordan set on the ground between them and stuffed it back into her bag. "Come on."

Except for the diner and the veterinary clinic, all the businesses were closed in the evening, and the town square was empty.

While Holly placed Skittles around the area to attract Marigold, Jordan used his slingshot to fire off any stones or bottle caps he came across.

He closed one eye and aimed at the hanging sign for the town store. The rock shot out of his slingshot and pinged off the sign, sending it swinging.

Ha! Nailed it!

"This is where Mr. Berkshire would've done his juggling," Holly said, standing on the large brick patio that everyone called the square. It was in the center of town

85

with a gazebo, a few small trees, and some strings of lights. "And Marigold would've been here with her pig."

Jordan turned in a circle, not surprised he didn't see any ghosts.

Holly climbed onto a bench for a better view. "I really thought she would be here, but there's no evidence she's been here at . . ." Holly went still, her gaze fixed on the grocery store window. "Did you see that?"

Jordan stiffened. "See what?"

"I saw someone." She hopped down from the bench and walked toward the grocery store.

"Inside the building?" If there was someone inside the store after closing, it could be a burglar. They might need to call his dad.

"They might've been inside, but I don't know. It was only a quick glance, like Annabelle said, and it was a shallow reflection person."

"A ghost?"

"That's what I'm thinking." Holly put away the bag of candy and cupped her hands over the window to peer inside.

Jordan looked inside, too, his eyes moving over the unlit aisles and packed shelves. He didn't see anyone . . . until he stepped back. Behind his reflection was another person.

He swallowed hard. "I think I found your ghost, Holly, and it's not Marigold." Three fifth graders came out of the alley on the far side of the street. It must've been one of their reflections Holly saw—a flicker as they moved between the buildings.

Holly turned to see Mike, Dan, and Colton. "Uh oh," she said under her breath.

Dan grinned. "Look what we found."

"Hey, Rat-cliffe!" Mike shouted, poking fun at Jordan's last name. "Catch!"

He threw a crumpled soda can at Jordan, and Jordan flinched, but the wind snatched the can out of the air before it could hit him.

The fifth graders laughed.

Holly stepped forward and shouted, "Don't throw things at my friend!"

"Or what, Casper?" Colton taunted.

Holly glared at him and drew her wooden sword, ready for a fight.

The boys laughed again, like a bunch of cackling hyenas. Dan threw his soda can at Holly, but the wind snatched that one too. It scraped and rolled across the square.

"You missed me!" Holly shouted. "And I'm not scared of you, you big bully."

Jordan was plenty scared enough for the both of them. He wanted to leave. Before they tied him to a pole by his shoelaces. Or worse.

Mike looked at Colton and then at Dan. "Who wants to play catch the rat? I bet I get to him first."

Jordan stepped back, his legs starting to tremble. Holly wanted to fight them back with her sword, but she wouldn't win, and then they would both end up tied to a pole.

The fifth graders broke into a run.

"Come on, Holly!" Jordan grabbed her arm and dragged her down the alley between the store and the bank.

"When we catch you, rat boy, we're gonna stuff you in a trash can where the rest of the rats like to hang out!" Mike hollered.

Jordan ran as fast as he could. He didn't want to have to climb out of a trash can, stinking like garbage and covered in eggshells and banana peels. He jumped over a stack of plastic milk crates, but Holly had to go around them because her legs were too short.

They were never going to outrun the fifth graders.

"The tree!" Jordan pointed to the tree up ahead with good climbing branches. But the lowest branch was too high for Holly. She wouldn't be able to reach it on her own. "I'll give you a boost, but you gotta drop the sword!"

Holly tossed the sword into the grass.

Jordan ducked down so she could climb on his shoulders and then lifted her up. *Please hurry,* he thought, as the fifth graders pounded closer.

"I got a branch!" she shouted.

Jordan ducked out from under her dangling legs and scrambled up the other side of the tree. They climbed as high as they could and straddled a thick branch—nose to nose, gulping air, Jordan's heart pounding so hard it might pop out of his chest at any moment.

The fifth graders gathered around the bottom of the tree and looked up.

"How do we keep them from climbing up after us?" Holly panted.

"I didn't think about that part."

"I have an idea," Holly whispered. "Do you still have your slingshot?"

"It's in my pocket."

Holly carefully slid one strap of her backpack from her shoulder so she could shift the bag to rest on the branch. She reached inside and pulled out the jumbo bag of Skittles. "How about a Skittle slingshot? That'll scare 'em off."

Mom had told Jordan never to shoot someone with his slingshot because he might accidentally hit them in the face and hurt them, but she didn't know about the bullies. If they came up here, they would push him and Holly out of the tree. Holly could get hurt. *He* could get hurt.

"Okay," he agreed. "Give me one."

Holly sprinkled a candy into his palm. Jordan positioned the Skittle in his slingshot.

Colton cupped his hands over his mouth and sang mockingly, "Rat boy and Casper, sittin' in a tree, k-i-s-s-i-n-g."

89

Jordan scowled. He would never kiss Holly. That was gross. "Leave us alone or you'll be sorry," he warned them.

"We got a trash can waiting for you." Mike grabbed the lower tree limb to pull himself up.

Jordan leaned his weight against the big limb behind him, closed one eye to aim, and released the Skittle. *Thwap!* The red blur hit Mike in the shoulder.

"Ow!" Mike let go of the limb and grabbed his shoulder. "He shot me with something."

Dan crouched to look at the ground. "It looks like a Skittle."

"We got a whole bag of those, and Jordan's a really good shot," Holly told them. "Better leave now."

"We're not scared of you." Dan moved toward the tree to climb up.

Jordan reloaded his slingshot with a blue Skittle. *Thwap!* He nailed Dan in the arm.

Dan jerked back, hugging his arm to his chest. "Hey! That really hurts!"

"We warned you," Holly said in a singsong voice.

Mike glared up at them. "Come on, guys, let's go. We'll get him back later."

Jordan waited with a third candy in his slingshot, but none of them made another grab for the tree. He watched as the bullies walked back toward the town square. Once they were out of sight, he slumped against the tree trunk at his back.

"That was brave," Holly told him.

"It was?"

"Yep. You deserve Skittles." She sprinkled some into his hand, and he tossed them into his mouth, enjoying the chewy tartness.

"How long should we stay up here?" he asked.

"Probably a while. Until we're sure they're gone." Holly tossed some candy into her mouth.

They munched their way through most of the bag of candy as they waited, saving a few pieces for the slingshot. When the sun started to drop behind the buildings, they climbed down and ran for Oma's house.

Oma's house was pretty and pink on the outside, but when the sun was going down, the windows reflected the orange-and-pink glow of the sky, and it reminded Holly of fire. Like there might be a fire-breathing dragon trapped inside, puffing on the glass.

The flowers in the flower bed were in full bloom, and there was pink and purple everywhere. Holly would ask if she could pick some flowers, but she was on a mission.

She opened the screen door and hurried into the inn, Jordan following close behind. "Oma?"

The older woman leaned out of the kitchen and smiled. "Hello, my sweet Holly. Just in time for fresh cookies."

Ooh. Cookies were one of Holly's favorite things in the whole world. After marshmallows, of course. Nothing was better than marshmallows.

"Smells like German biscuits!" Jordan said with excitement. "Strawberry jam?"

"Of course," Oma said.

German biscuits were Oma's special cookies, and everyone in town loved them. They were thin and buttery with strawberry jam in between—like a cookie sandwich—and a sweet glaze on top.

Oma stepped into the foyer in her flour-dusted apron. "I see someone tracked dirt inside."

Holly looked down at her dirty sneakers. Oops. She'd forgotten to take them off and put them by the wall when she came inside. "Sorry. I'll sweep it up."

"I know you will." Oma spread her arms. "But first I need my Holly hug."

Holly kicked off her shoes, placing them by the door, and then threw her arms around Oma's waist. "Hi, Oma."

"Hello, Schatzi."

Holly looked up. "What's that mean?"

"It means a lot of things. Little treasure, sweetheart, honey. All of which you are." Oma smiled. "My flour-covered Schatzi." She brushed flour smudges from Holly's cheeks and nose with her fingers.

Holly looked down at herself as she stepped back. Her overalls were covered in the flour from Oma's baking. She looked like a powdered donut.

Oma ran a hand over Jordan's hair and smiled. "I bet you two are hungry. Holly's momma called and said she didn't come home for dinner, and you didn't show up at the diner."

"We were trying to solve a mystery, and then we got stuck in a tree for a while 'cause some bullies were chasing Jordan," Holly said.

"Are these the same boys that were bothering you earlier this summer?" Oma looked from Holly to Jordan in concern. "I spoke with Mike's mother, and she said she would talk to him about his behavior."

"Well, it didn't work," Jordan grumbled.

"Maybe it's time to tell your father. He could talk to them and set them straight."

"No, I don't want him to know."

"Liebling—"

"Please, Oma, he'll only make it worse."

Oma sighed and pulled him into a hug. "You tell me if it happens again, and I'll handle it. And don't you let any of the lies those boys tell you make you feel bad about yourself."

Jordan hugged her back. "I won't."

"Good. Go wash up in the kitchen, and I'll warm up some leftovers from the icebox."

Holly followed Jordan into the kitchen and climbed onto the step stool to wash her hands alongside him. Oma grabbed a bowl from the fridge and placed it in the microwave.

"We'll need to call your parents, Holly, and let them know you're here so they can come pick you up," Oma said, grabbing the phone from the wall.

"Can't I spend the night here with Jordan?" Holly asked.

"It's Saturday, which means you and your family have church in the morning."

"But we go to the same church as you."

"True, but I don't have any church clothes for you to wear."

"Can we wash these?" Holly asked.

Oma considered her overalls and T-shirt. "If your parents say it's okay, then yes, I'll put them in the wash, and you can stay the night." The microwave beeped. "Jordy, grab the macaroni and cheese from the microwave and divide it between two bowls, please."

Holly plunked in a chair and eyed the cookies as she waited for Jordan to scoop their bowls of noodles.

"Here, Holly." He set a bowl in front of her and gave her a fork before sitting down beside her.

"Thanks." Holly bowed her head to say a prayer over her food the way Mom and Daddy had taught her. "Thank you, Jesus, for this food and for the person who made it. She's awesome. Amen."

"Yeah, amen," Jordan repeated.

Oma leaned a shoulder against the wall as she pressed the phone to her ear. "Cris, honey, it's Rosie. No need to search the town for your little one. She came bounding through the door with my grandson shortly before dark." She paused, listening, then said, "She's perfectly fine."

Holly forked a chunk of sausage and popped it into her mouth as she listened to see if she was going to get in trouble. The rule was *Be home before dark*, but this should count as home, too, shouldn't it?

"I know she had everyone worried, running off without telling anyone and not getting home for dinner," Oma said, and the look she gave Holly told her Daddy was upset.

Holly shrank a little lower in her chair. She didn't like it when Daddy was upset with her.

"You're welcome to come get her, but I'm more than happy to let her stay the night. I can wash her clothes and bring her to church with us in the morning," Oma said.

Please say yes, Daddy. Please say yes.

"All right. Give Emily and little Ginevieve my love." Oma said good night and hung up the phone. "Your daddy said you can sleep here tonight, but no more of this staying out so late you worry everyone."

Holly resisted the urge to jump up on her chair and do a happy dance. Sleepovers were the best! "No staying out so late. Got it."

"May I be excused from the table?" Jordan asked, halfway out of his chair.

"Clean up your dishes."

Jordan put his bowl and fork in the sink, and then grabbed the local phone book from the cubby on the wall by the phone. He opened it on the table, and then scooted his chair closer to Holly's. "Let's see if we can find her."

"Is this to do with your mystery?" Oma asked.

"Yeah. We're trying to find a woman named Marigold Miller," Jordan explained. "She used to be Mr. Berkshire's best friend, but she left a long time ago."

And turned into a ghost, Holly thought, but Jordan left that part out.

He flipped to the *M* section of the phone book and slid his finger down the page. "There are eight Millers, but none of them are Marigold."

"Is Miller her maiden name or her married name?" Oma asked. "Because that will make a difference."

Holly and Jordan looked at each other and asked at the same time, "Maiden name?"

"Her last name before she got married, when she was still a maiden."

"I think Miller was her name before," Holly said. "How do we figure out her married name?"

"Couldn't you ask this Mr. Berkshire?"

"No, talking about her makes him sad, 'cause then he thinks about when she left." Holly chased the last noodle around the bowl with her fork. "If we don't know her married name, how can we find her address?"

"She was a member of the Festival Funanza that used to travel around," Jordan said. "She had a pig that could perform tricks and stuff."

Oma tilted her head. "That sounds familiar. When we bought this house, it was full of old newspapers and flyers from whoever lived here before, and I saw some advertisements for that festival. I remember thinking it was a shame it wasn't around anymore. It would've been fun to attend."

Holly perked up in her chair. "Do you still have them?"

"They're upstairs in the attic. You two are welcome to look through them, but put everything away when you're done. I don't want a mess up there."

Holly jumped up from the table and put her dishes in the sink, ready to do some more research. They were going to find answers this time. She was sure of it.

"Holly, I need your clothes to wash. Your pillowcase dress is in the hall closet."

Oma had a long pillowcase with two armholes and a head hole cut into the fabric because Holly was always showing up like a walking mud monster and she didn't want to send her home dirty.

"Okay. Be back in a flash!" Holly dashed out of the room to change.

Jordan turned on his flashlight in the hallway. The light switch for the attic was a string hanging from a bulb all the way at the top, and he didn't want to walk up the steps in the dark.

The staircase was steep—more like climbing a mountain than walking up steps—and it was easy to trip. Plus, there were spiders. Lots and lots of spiders.

Holly stood beside him in her pillowcase, eyeing the door suspiciously. "What if it's haunted like Mr. Berkshire's attic?"

"I go up here all the time to help Oma bring boxes down. Christmas decorations and stuff. It's not haunted."

"You're sure there's nothing up there?"

"There was a bat up there last summer. And no, he wasn't a vampire."

"Vampires aren't real." Holly opened the door wide, peeked up the steps into the darkness, and then held out her hand. "Give me the flashlight. I'll go first."

Jordan passed it to her. He didn't want to get smacked in the face with a sticky spiderweb anyway. Holly crept up into the darkness, and he followed close behind, leaving the door open at the bottom for a little extra light. Or a quick escape if another bat snuck in through the vent.

"Aha! Found the light," Holly announced. She tugged on the string, and the lightbulb brightened the cluttered attic. She turned in a circle. "Wow, there's a lot of stuff."

"I remember boxes of old papers by the chimney. I bet those are what we need."

Holly dusted off an old pillow and tossed it on the floor to sit on, and then went over to the boxes. She grabbed a stack of newspapers and carried them over to her pillow. Jordan did the same.

"There's a lot to go through, and bedtime is in an hour," he said. They would never get through all these papers by then.

"We'll have to look fast, 'cause if I get time-out tomorrow, that means no more ghost hunting. And *that* means no helping Mr. Berkshire."

Jordan sifted through the crumply, old papers, blowing away dust and avoiding the silky blobs left behind by hatched spiders. Even though the webs were empty and old, the back of his neck itched as if dozens of baby spiders were creeping across it.

Halfway through his stack, Jordan sighed. "This is boring."

"I think it's cool. It's kind of like what your dad does as the sheriff. Finding clues and stuff." She tossed aside a newspaper and then gasped. "Look!" She held up a flyer so old the paper had gone yellow and brown. "Festival Funanza! There's Marigold and her pig."

Jordan squinted at the picture. "And she's wearing the hat from Mr. Berkshire's attic."

"That means we're close."

Except they weren't. Jordan had to go back for a second stack of papers before they found their next clue.

"Festival Funanza's very own Marigold Miller, pig trainer extra . . . or-din-air . . . pig trainer extraordinaire, marries local businessman, Rupert Riggle," Jordan read aloud. He set the paper down on top of the pile and grinned. "Her married last name is Riggle."

"I never would've guessed that."

"Me either."

"If he was a local business guy, does that mean he's from Stony Brooke?"

Jordan skimmed the rest of the article and then shrugged. "I don't know. It doesn't say, and there's a big water splotch in the middle."

"We should grab the local phone book and the big phone book. He and Marigold have to be in one of them."

The big phone book included numbers and addresses for people in the surrounding small towns. Jordan's dad called them "neighboring towns," but they were all pretty far away.

"I'll go get them," Jordan said, getting to his feet and sprinting down the steps.

Holly put away the stacks of papers they were done with. Except for the festival flyer. She decided to keep that one.

She snooped through a box of toys while she waited for Jordan to come back—probably the ones Oma kept here for him when he was little. Ooh, a metal slinky. She pulled it from the box and placed one end on each hand, moving her hands up and down to make it ripple. Cool.

Dropping it back in the box, she dug out a pair of Mickey Mouse ears. It was a view master. She and Gin had one of these. She put it up to her eyes like binoculars so she could see the pictures inside. She pulled a lever on the side, and the picture inside changed.

A growl made her lower the view master. A big cat scrambled up the steps, growling and hissing at something Holly couldn't see. He was so scared, his claws dug into the attic floor as he made a sharp turn, his tail puffed out like a stick of cotton candy.

"Kitty?"

Was that the cat Jordan got in a fight with? Maybe she shouldn't try to pet it.

A deep groan came from the hallway below. "Ooooaaah."

Holly's heart pitter-pattered in her chest as she stared down the steps. That sounded an awful lot like the spooky noises ghosts were known to make. And animals could see ghosts, even if they were invisible. She'd read that in her book.

"Ooooaaah," the groan came again, sending a shiver from Holly's neck all the way down to her littlest toe.

Jordan said the attic wasn't haunted, but there was definitely something spooky coming down the hall, and it was coming straight for the attic.

Holly crouched and held tight to the Mickey Mouse view master. She wasn't going to be bullied by a ghost into hiding.

A white figure came into view—like a spirit trapped beneath a white sheet. Jordan must've tried to catch it, but it slipped away with the sheet!

"Ooooaaah!" it said, waving an arm around.

"You don't scare me!" Holly shouted, and she hurled the view master. It clunked the ghost in the head, and he stumbled back, falling to his butt on the floor.

Ha! I got him!

"Ow, Holly!" The ghost raised an arm to rub at his head.

Wait a minute . . . Holly knew that voice. She bounced down the steps and grabbed the sheet, giving it a hard tug. It fell away to reveal Jordan sitting on the floor.

"Jordan, that wasn't funny."

"Was too. Until you hit me." He rubbed at the red spot on his forehead. "Why can't you throw that good when we're playing catch?"

"It was a really good throw."

"You thought I was a real ghost."

Holly grinned. "You were pretty convincing with your uoOOooh."

They both laughed.

A door opened down the hall, and a man whose bald head was as shiny as the moon leaned out. "What's going on out here?"

"Sorry, Mr. Evans. We'll be quieter," Jordan promised. He waited for Oma's guest to close his door before saying, "I got the phone books. Let's go see what we can find."

They headed back upstairs. Holly looked through the local phone book for anyone named Riggle, and Jordan looked through the big one. It took a while, but he finally found it.

"Rupert and Marigold Riggle. They live in Apple Ridge," he said.

Holly was a little disappointed that they didn't live in Stony Brooke, but Apple Ridge wasn't too far. "Daddy goes there sometimes to drop off his extra books. I bet he'll take us."

"We should ask him tomorrow."

Oma appeared at the bottom of the steps. "Children, it's time for bed."

"Five more minutes?" Jordan asked.

"We're not negotiating. It's time for bed now. And brush your teeth first."

"Okay." Jordan looked up at the lightbulb on the ceiling. "Turn it off together and run down the steps?"

Holly clicked on the flashlight. "Let's do it."

Jordan pulled the light switch string, and the attic went dark. The two of them raced down the steps and into the light of the hallway, leaving the door open for the cat hiding upstairs in one of the boxes.

As soon as Sunday school let out the next morning, Holly took Gin's hand and led her through the stream of people flowing toward the front doors as she searched for Mom and Dad.

She found them standing in the lobby with the mean woman from the cemetery.

Oh no.

Annabelle had found her parents. Holly was headed for trouble, and there was nothing she could do about it. Time-out for life.

"Do you know where your daughter was yesterday?" Annabelle demanded, hands on her hips.

Daddy looked at Mom before asking, "Which one? We have two."

"The red-haired one. Says she's nine years old."

"They're twins."

Annabelle huffed. "Of course they are. The one who runs around with that boy."

Daddy tucked his hands into the pockets of his pants. "That would be Holly."

"She was at the cemetery, attacking people like me who were there to visit the graves of their loved ones," Annabelle explained.

"That doesn't sound like our daughter."

"She stabbed me in the back with a sword."

Daddy's eyes found Holly in the lobby, and she wanted to shrink down into the carpet like those kids from the movie *Honey, I Shrunk the Kids*. Daddy turned his attention back to Annabelle. "This sword wouldn't happen to be a blunt wooden toy, would it?"

"That is *not* the point. The point is, your daughter was disrespectful."

"You're right. I'll talk to her so nothing like this happens again."

Annabelle huffed. "Talking won't cut it. She needs to see some consequences for her behavior. At the very least, take that weapon away from her before she hurts someone."

"It's not a weapon. It's a toy. She couldn't hurt someone with it if she tried. And to be honest, I'm surprised you would feel so threatened by a nine-year-old playing pretend."

Mom put her hand on Daddy's arm. "Thank you for bringing this situation to our attention, Annabelle. We'll deal with it."

"See that you do." Annabelle pulled her purse up on to her shoulder. "And you should know, your nine-year-old is out ghost hunting with her *toys*. That's dangerous business for a child. I would keep a better eye on her, if I were you."

She stomped away.

Mom shook her head. "Well, she's quite the difficult soul."

Daddy frowned. "Did she say ghost hunting?"

"I believe she did."

Jordan came up beside Holly and whispered, "Are you in trouble?"

"I don't know yet," Holly whispered back.

Daddy motioned Holly and Gin to join them. "Girls."

Holly dragged her feet as she walked over, stalling to avoid consequences. She didn't want to be in trouble. She really didn't. "Daddy, I told her I was sorry. It was all a mistake. And I didn't poke her hard. I wasn't trying to hurt her."

Daddy crouched in front of them. "I know, Jelly Bean. But cemeteries aren't for playing. And you need to understand that not all adults remember *how* to play. They don't have imaginations like you anymore, and because of that, some of them are very serious people. Like Annabelle. You need to ask adults if they want to play with you before you go trying to sword fight them."

"But I wasn't trying to sword fight her. I really thought she was a ghost."

Gin gasped. "You saw a ghost?"

Daddy opened his mouth to say something, when an old woman rushed up to Mom and shouted, "Oh thank goodness, Emily! I was hoping you would still be here."

"What's wrong, Stella?" Mom asked.

"I was sewing, and I got up to get a drink, and when I came back, Angel was eating my needle and thread. She swallowed it before I could get to her. I don't know what to do."

Mom took her hands to calm her. "It'll be okay. Bring her to the clinic, and I'll meet you there. We'll do an X-ray and see what we're dealing with, but your kitty should be fine."

The woman nodded. "Okay. Okay, I'll be there in less than twenty minutes." She ran back out the doors she'd come through.

Mom turned back to them. "I'm sorry, I know we have a lot to talk about today, but I need to go."

Daddy stood and gave her a kiss. "We'll manage. Go save a life."

Mom bent down in front of the girls. "I'm sorry I have to work again. But I do have this for you." She pulled a picture from her purse and handed it to Holly. "Both the mommy horse and baby horse I helped yesterday are healthy and happy."

"Aww," Holly and Gin said together as they looked at the picture of the baby horse lying in the grass.

"I love you both. Listen to your daddy." Mom kissed them both on the forehead, then gave Jordan a kiss, too, before standing. She called out to someone as she left and asked for a ride to the vet clinic.

Daddy sat down on the floor in the middle of the church lobby, which was almost empty of people, and patted the carpet beside him. "Sit with me."

Holly and Jordan sat down across from him, while Gin plopped into his lap.

"What's got you kids thinking about ghosts?" he asked.

"I asked Mr. Berkshire why he locks his attic, 'cause I thought it was weird. Nobody else lives there, and his dog can't open doors. He said there are old ghosts up there, and it would be better if they stay there, and that's why he locks it," Holly explained.

"And when we found him in the attic the next morning, he was telling us about his friend Marigold, and he said he was being haunted," Jordan added.

"So we thought maybe the ghost escaped when he unlocked the door, and we've been trying to find her so we can tell her to stop haunting him."

"Ah, I see," Daddy said. "So the cemetery and all the running around has been to help Mr. Berkshire?"

Holly nodded. "She's making him sad. If she would stop haunting him, then he would feel better."

Daddy smiled. "You have a beautiful heart, my sweet girl. I'm proud of you for that. But when grown-ups talk about old ghosts, they don't mean *real* ghosts. They're talking about old memories, things they've said or done that still bother them, that still *haunt* them years later. Like a ghost might, if they were anything more than stories."

Holly frowned. "But Annabelle said she saw her sister after she died. Did she lie?"

Daddy thought about that for a second. "No, she probably believes what she told you is true. Sometimes . . . people miss someone they've lost so much that they think they see their ghost because it makes them feel better, like that person is still here even when they're not."

"Like a mirage?" Jordan asked.

"A little bit like that, yes."

Gin looked up at Daddy. "What's a mirage?"

"Do you remember in *Fievel Goes West,* when the mouse is lost in the desert, all alone, and he thinks he sees his family?" Daddy asked her.

"Yeah, but it's not really his family."

"That's a mirage. He sees his family, the thing he wants more than anything else, and he believes they're real, but his eyes are playing tricks on him."

"That means . . . ghosts aren't real?" Holly asked, not sure she was ready to believe that.

Daddy thought for a second before answering. "You know God loves each and every one of us, right?"

"Yeah."

"He knows us before we're even born. He knows the number of hairs on our head, and we don't even know that about ourselves. If God sees and knows that much, do you think He would forget about us when we die and leave us floating around in a world we no longer belong in?"

Holly puckered her lips to one side. "I guess not. But what about the Holy Ghost?"

Daddy smiled. "That's a different matter entirely. The Holy Ghost—or Holy Spirit, some people call Him—is a part of God, and God is very much alive. When we decide to follow Jesus, the Holy Ghost comes to live inside us." Daddy pressed a hand to his chest. "He keeps us connected to God and helps guide us."

Gin clapped her hands together. "Follow Jesus where? Is He going on an adventure? Can I go too? Can we bring snacks?"

"Life with Jesus is always an adventure, Gingersnap. What I mean when I say follow Him is . . . we invite Jesus into our hearts, and we follow His example by loving others, being kind and honest, and offering forgiveness."

"Oh. Am I kind and honest?"

"Both of my girls are," Daddy said.

"So ghosts only exist in movies and books?" Jordan asked.

Daddy nodded. "That's right."

Jordan folded his arms and smiled. "Told you there was no such thing as ghosts, Holly."

Holly threw him a scowl. "I'm still not sure. I wanna go to the address we found, and then we'll know."

"What address?" Daddy asked.

Jordan pulled a crumpled paper from the pocket of his jeans. "I wrote it down. This is where the gh- . . . I mean, where Marigold used to live, and we were gonna see if her ghost was there so we could talk to her."

Daddy took the paper from him. "Apple Ridge is only a fifteen-minute drive, and I need to drop off some extra book donations anyway. If we go here and talk to this couple, will that help you understand what I'm trying to teach you, Holly? That ghosts aren't real?"

"Maybe."

But she was betting Daddy would be the one who learned something, because Marigold had to be a ghost. It was the only thing that made sense. She and Mr. Berkshire used to be best friends, and best friends were forever. They *always* said sorry and made up. If Marigold was alive, they would still be friends.

Holly watched out the window as trees buzzed by the car, her ghost-hunting kit hugged to her stomach. Daddy might be convinced ghosts were imaginary, but until she knew for sure, she wanted to be prepared.

She even had her book so she could show Daddy the facts once she caught Marigold. Wouldn't he be surprised!

The car turned into the driveway of an old house, and butterflies fluttered around in Holly's belly. She was a little excited *and* a little scared. They were going to find Marigold here, she knew that, but what would she be like?

Angry ghosts turned into polter-ghosts, and Marigold had been so mad, she threw her hat at Mr. Berkshire when she left. Would she still be angry?

"We're here," Daddy said.

Holly unbuckled her seat belt and scooted forward to see the house through the front window. Her jaw dropped to her chin in wonder. "Wow."

It was a cream stone castle with red around the windows and bricks along the bottom, and it was covered with green ivy. The vines grew wild in every direction, like they were ropes trying to drag the house down into the earth.

Daddy climbed out of the car and opened the back door. He leaned in to help Gin unbuckle her seat belt. "Leave your Polly Pockets in the car so you don't lose it."

"Okay, Daddy." Gin set her miniature doll set on the floor and took Daddy's hand so he could help her out.

Jordan slid out next, and Holly scooted after him, glad the seats weren't as hot as they were after church. The summer sun always turned the backseat into molten lava. Sometimes the seat was so hot, her body stuck to it like the sticky glue on an envelope.

Holly scooted out of the backseat and shrugged her backpack straps over her shoulders. Her eyes traced the massive tree that stretched high into the sky over the car. Its branches were like claws trying to snatch clouds out of the sky.

It was almost as spooky as the Watcher Tree in the woods where she and Jordan played. Even the ancient brown bark curled outward, like it might reach for her next.

"Daddy, there's a monster," Gin whimpered, drawing Holly's attention to the dry stone fountain in the center of the driveway.

A stone beast stood tall in the middle of the fountain, mouth open to show its sharp fangs.

"His teeth are longer than my fingers," Jordan whispered.

Daddy scooped Gin up. "It's only a gargoyle, baby girl. Nothing to worry about."

"He's staring at me with his scary eyes."

Daddy stroked her back. "He's made of stone. He can't hurt you."

Gin laid her head on his shoulder. "Okay."

Holly studied the gargoyle as everyone else walked toward the front porch. He was definitely scary, but he also looked a little lonely and sad. Like everything else here.

This place had to be haunted—from the water fountain to the treetops. Holly grabbed her ghost-detecting doohickey from her backpack and joined the others on the porch.

Daddy pressed the doorbell button, and music came from inside the house—*ding, dang, ding dooooong*. The dong was so deep and long, Holly could feel it in her chest.

"That's . . . quite a doorbell," Daddy said.

A few minutes later, the door opened from the other side, and a thin woman with long white hair stood in the doorway. She stared over their heads as she said, "Yes?"

"Are you Mrs. Riggle?" Daddy asked.

The woman cocked her head toward him like a bird. "Who's asking?"

Holly followed the woman's eyes to the gargoyle fountain behind them. What was she looking at back there?

"My name is Cristopher Cross. I'm sorry to bother you, but my children were hoping to meet you."

The woman's eyebrows lifted. "Meet *me*?"

Holly tugged on the bottom of Daddy's shirt and whispered, "Daddy, she's not Marigold." She was too old to be the ghost they were looking for, and she wasn't even a ghost at all. She looked as solid as Annabelle in the cemetery, and Holly wasn't going to make that mistake again.

"Marigold?" the old woman repeated. "I haven't been called that in ages. Everyone calls me Goldie. I'm sorry I don't recognize the name Cross. Do we know each other?"

Holly thought that was a weird question. Couldn't she tell by looking at them that she didn't know them?

"No, we've never met," Daddy said. "We're from a town called Stony Brooke. It's about fifteen miles south of here."

"Yes, I . . . I haven't been there in . . . fifty or so years, but I remember it. It's a small, quiet community. Kind people. I had a friend there . . . once upon a time."

"Mr. Berkshire?" Jordan asked.

117

The old woman angled her head in Jordan's direction. "Yes, how did you know that? Do you know John?"

"We've been helping him clean his house and mow his grass. Since he's got a bad heart."

"Oh, John. I always warned him to take better care of himself." She pressed a hand to her chest, and that was when Holly noticed the necklace she was wearing. It was the same silver locket from the painting in Mr. Berkshire's attic, and . . .

Holly wiggled the flyer from her pocket and unfolded it. She squinted at the photo of Marigold and her pig and then back at the old woman's locket. It was the same necklace in the flyer.

But this didn't make sense.

"You were Mr. Berkshire's best friend?" Holly asked.

"We were a bit more than friends, but yes," the old woman answered.

"Then why would you leave him all alone? Best friends don't do that."

"Holly Marie," Daddy said sharply. "That is enough."

"But Daddy, she shouldn't have—"

"I said *enough*."

Holly snapped her teeth together. She was so mad, she felt hot all over, so hot she could've ignited like a marshmallow over a fire. She could help Mr. Berkshire be happy again by fixing a ghost problem, but she couldn't fix a bad best friend.

Daddy softened his voice when he turned back to Marigold. "I'm so sorry. We'll leave you to enjoy the rest of your day in peace."

"There's no reason to be sorry," Marigold said. "Your daughter's right. I shouldn't have left the way I did. It's one of my biggest regrets."

Holly's head popped up. "You mean you wish you could take it back?"

"Yes . . . and no." She stepped to one side of the doorway and held out a hand. "Please come in. If you have time, of course."

"We have plenty of time today," Daddy said, stepping inside the house. Jordan and Holly followed.

Marigold closed the door and slid a hand along the wall as she walked past them. "The den is up here on the left. There's a light switch on the right wall if you need it. I'm afraid I don't have much use for lights these days."

Holly and Jordan glanced at each other, curious, before Jordan asked, "Are you blind?"

"I am. I wasn't always, but I had a brain tumor years ago that stole my vision, and it never came back." She stopped walking and gestured toward the doorway to the den. "We should be here."

"Wow, how'd you do that?" Jordan asked.

Marigold smiled. "Lots of practice. Trust me, I've run into my fair share of walls and chairs. Could I get you all something to drink?"

"Do you have blue Kool-Aid?" Gin asked. "Blue's my favorite."

"I'm sorry, I don't."

"That's okay. Next time we come visit, I'll ask Mommy if we can bring you some. We'll share it."

"That's very thoughtful."

Daddy turned on the living room light and set Gin down. "Kids, on the couch. Don't touch anything that doesn't belong to you."

Holly grunted unhappily and plopped on the couch with Jordan and Gin. She wanted to explore the old house and find out its secrets. She would bet Mr. Berkshire's attic wasn't the only attic with interesting stuff in it.

Marigold slid her hand over the back of a chair, down the arm, and over the cushion before sitting. "To answer the question your daughter asked outside, I do and don't wish I could take back what happened between me and John all those years ago. I wish I could undo the pain my leaving must've caused him. At the time, I was angry and hurt, and I acted without thinking."

"But you could've come back when you weren't angry anymore," Holly said.

"I was scared he wouldn't want me back, that he wouldn't forgive me for the hurtful things I said and did the day I left."

"Best friends always forgive each other. All you have to do is say you're sorry," Holly explained.

"Things can be a little more complicated for adults, sweetheart," Daddy said.

Why? Saying sorry wasn't *that* hard.

"You see, by the time the anger and hurt started to fade away, I'd met Rupert. Like me, he wanted a family, and he was a good man. We got married, and we have three grown children. That's why I wouldn't take back what happened between me and John. I love our children, and they only exist because I met Rupert."

"So you left and never went back to see Mr. Berkshire again?" Jordan asked.

Marigold shook her head. "A part of my heart has always loved John, even after what happened between us, and I know we could've been happy together if things had gone differently. But I also loved my husband, and there was only room for one of them in my life. I chose Rupert."

"Where's your husband now?" Jordan asked.

"He died five years ago," Marigold said, her voice heavy with sadness. "I miss him every day. He's gone, the kids have moved on with lives of their own, and . . . some days this house feels like a lonely tomb."

Holly looked around at all the decorations. It was awfully fancy for a tomb. Not that she knew much about tombs. But it was big and echoey, and a person could only talk to her own echo for so long before she got bored and lonely.

"I'm sorry," Daddy said. "I can only imagine how hard these past five years have been for you." He crouched by Marigold's chair. "I hope I'm not being too intrusive by asking this, but have you considered reaching out to John?"

Marigold shook her head. "I couldn't. He would hang up the phone the moment he realized it was me."

"No he wouldn't," Holly said, sliding off the couch. She came to sit on the sliver of chair by Marigold's legs. "He misses you."

"I doubt that."

"He has all kinds of stuff of yours in the attic. Paintings and hats. He kept the door locked 'cause he said being around that stuff hurts, and not 'cause he's mad at you. He said he doesn't blame you," Jordan said.

"He even came looking for you," Holly added. "But then he saw you were married, so . . . he went home, and he's been sad and lonely ever since. All he has is a dog, and he's as grumpy as he is lazy."

Marigold blinked her tear-filled eyes. "Oh, John. I never knew he came looking for me. He's alone? He never married?"

Holly shook her head, then remembered Marigold was blind. "Nope."

"It sounds like you two might have a second chance," Daddy said.

"It's been so long, I can't imagine . . ." She touched her lips. "He wouldn't even recognize me now. I'm so old and wrinkled."

"That's okay. Mr. Berkenshire's old too," Gin said, and Daddy smiled.

"I don't even know what I look like anymore. I haven't seen my reflection in years," Marigold said.

"You have really pretty blue eyes, and your hair is like a waterfall of snow," Holly told her. "And you have a freckle on your lip that Mom calls sunshine kisses."

Marigold patted Holly's leg. "Thank you." She grabbed a folded cloth from the table beside her and dabbed at her tears. "I'm not certain how I would get to Stony Brooke. I can't drive anymore, and it feels wrong to ask one of my children to drive me to see the man I loved before their father."

"We'll drive you," Daddy said.

"I couldn't ask you to do that."

"You didn't. I offered. Besides, I'm a bit of a book fanatic, and I love stories where people come together in the end. Now I get to be a part of one. Let me help you up."

Marigold felt around at the air until she found his hands and let Daddy help her to her feet. "All right. I'm ready for our adventure."

Daddy parked the car beside the falling-apart truck in Mr. Berkshire's driveway and turned off the engine. "We're here."

Marigold released a shaky breath and touched the passenger door. "I wish I could see it. Would you describe it to me?"

"It's a big house, sort of grayish with little white spots, with a wraparound porch and a metal thingy of a rooster on the roof," Holly said as she unhooked her seat belt. "What is that thing anyway?"

"It's called a weathervane," Daddy answered. "It helps measure the direction of the wind. They're mostly decorative nowadays, but they were important back when travel was done by sea and the wind affected ship sails."

"Everything sounds the same, except the house used to be all white." Marigold smiled. "I can picture it in my mind. We planted sunflowers together by the front fence."

There were no sunflowers now, but maybe they died or Mr. Berkshire ripped them out because they haunted him like the stuff in the attic.

Holly started to open her door. "Can I tell Mr. Berkshire he has company, Daddy?"

"Go ahead, baby."

Holly hopped out and ran through the grass to the porch. Mr. Berkshire was usually sitting on the porch with his dog, but not today.

The front door was open like it always was, so Holly poked her head inside. "Mr. Berkshire? Are you awake?"

Sometimes old people fell asleep in the middle of the day. Probably because they were bored. Holly would be bored to sleep, too, if she couldn't run around and play.

"It's your friend Holly!"

Mr. Berkshire appeared at the top of the steps. "I wasn't expecting you to come clean today. Don't churchgoers have some rule about no work on Sundays?"

"We're not here to clean."

The steps creaked as he came down them. "Here for a visit then?"

"Sort of." Holly tucked her fingers into the back pockets of her overalls. "See, the thing is, I thought you had a ghost haunting your attic, so Jordan and I decided to find her and tell her to leave you alone. But when we found her, she wasn't exactly a ghost."

Mr. Berkshire frowned. "What would give you the idea I had a ghost in my attic?"

"You said you were haunted."

He made a silent "Oh" with his lips. "So I did, but I didn't mean there are spirits floating around my house."

"Daddy explained. But . . . we found her."

"Found who?"

"Your *not* ghost. Marigold. She's outside."

Mr. Berkshire gripped the staircase railing, his legs going wobbly at the knees. "Did you say she's out- . . . outside?"

"In the car."

"You brought her here?"

Holly nodded slowly. He didn't sound very happy that his best friend was outside in his driveway. Was he still mad at her? Should they take her home?

Mr. Berkshire sank onto the steps and shook his head. "She shouldn't be here. She has a family. A husband."

Holly sat down beside him. "She has grown-up kids, but her husband died a long time ago. She's been really lonely, like you."

"She has?"

"Yep, and no one should have to be lonely. I know she hurt your feelings, but she's really sorry, and you should forgive her. Then you won't be alone anymore, and you can be happy."

Mr. Berkshire stared at her. "You did this for me?"

"Jordan and Daddy helped. And Gin was there too."

"She really wants to see me?"

"Yep." Holly paused, then added, "Well, sort of."

126

"I don't know what to do. I don't have anything nice to wear." He ran a hand over his stained shirt and then over his beard. "I haven't trimmed my beard in years. I can't let her see me like . . . wait a minute. Did you say she only *sort of* wants to see me?"

"She can't actually see you. She's blind."

"Blind?"

"Yeah, she has one of those folding sticks for when she walks, and she's really good with it. She almost walks better than me, and I can see my feet," Holly said.

Mr. Berkshire drew a deep breath and let it out. "I'll meet her on the porch so she doesn't have to try to get around all my things."

"I'll go get her." Holly hopped up and dashed back to the car. "He's ready, Daddy!"

Daddy got out of the car and came around to open Marigold's door. "My hand is here if you need it."

Marigold took his hand, and Daddy helped her to her feet. She unfolded her cane and tapped one end against the ground in front of her. "I can't believe I'm doing this. I'm eighty years old, but I feel as nervous and excited as a schoolgirl."

"Let me walk you up. The sidewalk and steps are a little uneven," Daddy said, taking her by the elbow. "You kids stay here, and Holly, keep an eye on your sister."

Holly wanted to argue, but she knew better. Jordan got out of the car to stand beside her, leaving Gin alone in the backseat with her Polly Pocket.

Mr. Berkshire came out onto the porch, smoothing his beard with his hands. It was still as bushy as a raccoon tail. He stopped and stared at Marigold, his mouth slightly open. "H-hey there, Marigold. It's been a long time."

Daddy helped Marigold onto the porch.

She stood in front of Mr. Berkshire. "Hi, John. It's nice to hear your voice. I'm sorry for how I must look. It's hard to keep up appearances when I can't see myself."

"You look beautiful as ever."

"Thank you."

"Here, I have a seat for you. We, uh . . ." Mr. Berkshire quickly cleaned off a bench, tossing the junk off to the side. "We can sit and talk for a while."

"That would be nice. Mr. Cross, do you mind helping me find the chair?"

Daddy guided her to the bench, and she sat, leaning her cane against the wall.

"Are you thirsty?" Mr. Berkshire asked. "I can get you a drink. I have cold water and, uh, warm water."

Marigold laughed. "I'm all right."

"All right. Good. Me too." Mr. Berkshire rubbed his hands together nervously and then sat down beside her on the bench. "I really am glad you're here. Would you . . . tell me about your life? Holly said you've got kids."

"Do you really want to hear about my kids?"

"I do. I want to hear everything."

She smiled and placed her hand on his arm. "Me too."

"I'll give you two some privacy. Ms. Marigold, let me know when you're ready to go home, and I'll drive you," Daddy said.

"Thank you so much," Marigold said. "For everything. I can't begin to tell you how much this means to me."

Mr. Berkshire cleared his throat. "To both of us."

Holly turned to Jordan and whispered, "We did it."

"Did what?"

"Solved the ghost mystery *and* brought two best friends back together." She crossed her arms and lifted her chin proudly. "We're pretty good at this."

Jordan kicked a pebble, sending it bouncing down the sidewalk. "I guess so."

"Then why do you sound sad?"

He shrugged. "I don't think it's fair. She left and had a whole life, and he's been all alone with no friends all this time." He stared at the ground as he mumbled, "I don't want you to leave like she did, 'cause then *I'll* be the one all alone with no friends."

Holly frowned. "I wouldn't do that."

"You said you wanna travel and be an explorer when you grow up. That means you have to leave Stony Brooke."

"We go on adventures together. I wouldn't leave you behind."

Jordan looked over at her. "Promise?"

She held out her little finger. "Pinky promise." And a pinky promise was no ordinary promise. It lasted forever. "We're best friends, and best friends help each other and stick together."

Jordan lifted his hand. "Best friends forever?"

Holly hooked her pinky around his. "Best friends forever."

Keep an eye out for the next installment of
MYSTERIES, MISCHIEF, and MARSHMALLOWS

About the Author

Jesus and laughter have brought C.C. Warrens through some very difficult times in life, and she weaves both into every story she writes, creating a world of breath-stealing intensity, laugh-out-loud humor, and a sparkle of hope. Writing has been a slowly blossoming dream inside her for most of her life until one day it spilled out onto the pages that would become her first published book.

If she's not writing, she's attempting to bake something—however catastrophic that might be—or she's enjoying the beauty of the outdoors with her husband.

CONTACT
Facebook: ccwarrens
Instagram: c.c._warrens
TikTok: c.c._warrens
Website: ccwarrens.com